When Love Meets Lies

Stephanie Cross

Copyright © 2021 Stephanie Cross (SLEC Publications). All rights reserved.

No part of this publication may be reproduced, distributed or transmitted in any form or by any means, including photocopying, recording or other electronic or mechanical methods, without the prior written permission of the publisher, except in the case of brief quotations embodied in reviews and certain other non-commercial uses permitted by copyright law.

Disclaimer: The characters in this book are entirely fictional. Any resemblance to actual persons living or dead is entirely coincidental.

ISBN: 978-1-9999749-2-3

First Edition

STEPHANIE CROSS

This book is dedicated to all the silly sausages!

CHAPTER 1

I roll over in bed still half asleep, the white sheets cocooned around my body. I stretch out to the other side to feel his touch and his warmth, in order to make my journey out of dreamland into reality more bearable. The space where he should be lying is empty. I clutch at the bed sheet covering the mattress where his body should be, in the hope that it will bring him back to this empty space. Every morning for the past six months I have felt his warm skin on my skin. That feeling of someone being there every day, morning and night has provided me with the stability and comfort that I have craved for so long. It feels like a dream, yet today the dream is shattered as I toss and turn in an empty bed wondering where he has gone.

Beep. Beep. Beep. The alarm goes off. It's 5am, and as much as I wish to stay in bed, work is calling. Despite being awoken at such an ungodly hour and him not there, it is made bearable by the fact I am getting up to do something I genuinely enjoy. Okay it doesn't require me to use my real talent of drawing but it does allow me to get closer to nature.

As I stretch and yawn and try to come alive, oh Dolly Parton, your songs still get me going on a cold February morning, I feel someone watching me from the end of the bed. I wipe the sleep from my eyes with the back of my hands to get a clearer look at who is waiting for me at the foot of my safe and comfy bed.

'Good morning gorgeous,' says the figure.

The outline is still a little bit fuzzy, so I rub my eyes again to see who it is. He walks around to my side of the bed and plants a sweet kiss on the top of my head and the warm feeling I missed from this morning's snuggle in bed returns.

'I thought I would surprise you with a nice cup of tea this morning.'

He doesn't need to get up at this time to go to his work but he has, in fact he has been getting up the same time I have since we moved in together, in his flat, six months ago. Ever since we have been together, he has always put me first. I just hope this isn't just a 'honeymoon phase' he's in or he holds it against me later on in our relationship. The guilt gets me every time, no one has been this good to me before, well maybe there was one but that ended in disaster.

'Thanks Laurence. That's exactly what I need to wake me up this morning.'

'Anything for my beautiful one. Now don't take too long drinking that tea, people need to be dazzled by your amazingness at work today.'

This life with Laurence was never meant to have happened but it did; and so effortlessly too. When he first got in contact with me after my less than perfect exit from Australia and Ryan's betrayal, I thought he would be the best person to have a bit of fun with, no strings attached and definitely nothing serious. I have been at the receiving end of people expressing lust towards me rather than love, so I thought it would make a change to turn the tables and have a go at being the one to call the shots. Laurence clearly spelled out to me in the text message he sent me before my flight back home that he liked me and I thought it would be easy to just switch off my emotions and enjoy toying with his affections when I returned to the U.K. And my god was I a bitch and a half to him; taking my time to respond to his messages or not responding at all, doing no-shows and one-word replies, it was like the devil had taken over. If I was him, I would've told me to fuck right off and blocked my number instead of persisting with getting a first date.

Yet here I am several months later, cosying up to this beautiful blond bombshell and calling him my boyfriend. When I finally agreed to meet him for our first date after several cancellations on my part, something about him just made me feel safe and secure. We had so much more in common than just physical attraction, as we ended up talking for hours and hours not needing to touch or kiss each other to pass the time. The more we talked, the less confident I became at just seeing Laurence as a quick fling, my heart couldn't do it. Even at the end of the date when I tried to force myself on him and give him a passionate kiss, he pushed me away telling me he wanted to do things properly. At this point my Ice Queen act well and truly melted. He saw our potential relationship as something 'special' he wanted to develop slowly. Despite hearing similar words like this before and being deeply let down, this time something inside told me this guy was genuine. Maybe this time it would work, and the only way it would work is if I stopped thinking about myself and started thinking of how the two of us can make the best of our relationship in this crazy world we live in.

Not only has my relationship status changed since arriving back in the U.K., my working life has changed too. I am no longer a slave to the office and instead run a market stall selling plants and flowers. In fact I am due to open my first shop in a few weeks' time, it will be called the Lemon Tree in honour of my Granddad Shane. Just a month after I landed he unfortunately passed away. It's his inheritance that has given me the chance to open up my own shop, and as he was infamously known for always having lemon sherbets in his back pocket, I thought it was right to make some reference to them in my business as a thank you.

As I slurp my tea and let the warm liquid heat my body up to deal with the cold day ahead, I take a moment to reflect on everything that has happened to me in the past year, the good, the bad and the ugly. I feel the scar on my arm, memories triggered as to the journey of love and pain I went through to get to this moment of contentment with Laurence. Yet it also reminds me of what could have been. What if I had stayed in Australia, what if I hadn't overreacted to Ryan having a girl turn up in his room, I mean he looked as shocked as I did that she was there so maybe it was more innocent than I gave him credit for. What if we did stay together?

The what if questions dissipate as Laurence takes the mug away from my hand and places it on the bedside cabinet, pulls back the duvet and begins to cover my arm in kisses as he slowly lifts me out of bed, meaning I have no choice but to get up and face another day of adventures.

CHAPTER 2

It may be only two degrees outside but it is one hundred and two degrees inside. This lecture theatre is absolutely roasting. I desperately want to strip down to my jocks, yet the rest of the audience seem to be wrapped up in their thickest woollen jumpers. It's probably because most of the audience are over fifty-five and you know what old people are like, it could be thirty-five degrees outside and they still wear three layers because they think it's cold. Even coming from a place where it is often hot doesn't mean I can cope with it well. It probably doesn't help that Mum seems to be filling the room with a whole load of hot air as well, about how you can maximise your happiness with a youthful relationship. The audience are hanging on to her every word and Chad seems to be enjoying it as well.

'Your Mum is pretty good about this relationship stuff ay. I might try and use some of these tips she's offering up.'

Chad hasn't mastered the art of learning how to whisper, which has meant that the whole row behind me and Sir Stinkalot sitting next to me, seriously I think the last time this guy washed must have been 1959, all make shushing signals just in case they might miss one piece of vital information in order to become a 'youthful lover.'

'Chad.' I whisper back, 'you need to keep your voice down.'

He also needs to stop stuffing that popcorn in his face and learn to close his mouth as all I can see is a mouthful of yellow going round and round whenever I glance over at him.

'Sorry Dude,' he says again in a shouting whisper causing several invisible daggers to be thrown at us from the row behind. This time I pull an invisible zip across my mouth to tell Chad he really needs to button it and he gets the message and shuts up. I try not to be too harsh on the guy as he has had a tough time recently, and the fact he has agreed to come to London with me has made the move abroad for me a little bit easier.

I was meant to be here in the U.K. six months earlier but because of fucking 'Larrykins', Mum's pet and occasional lover, she had to postpone her lectures in Oxford so she could look after him, because the imbecile managed to break his leg tripping over his stepper at a step aerobics class. I mean what kind of twenty-eight-year-old man goes to a fucking step aerobics class anyway. I am sure he could cope on his own, it was just the one leg that was broken; the other one still works. According to Mother dearest, he needs emotional support as well as physical support as he felt so low not being able to be part of the Madame Butterfly performance anymore due to his injury. I don't believe he's depressed, he has the starring role of being a little Madam every day at Mum's house.

It doesn't matter that I am her son and I need emotional support because she postponed the trip – the trip I need to make to have my only chance at love. Despite explaining this to Mother it is apparently I who needs to get a grip, not Larry. As she had booked the tickets I decided to wait the extra six months rather than go earlier. I wasn't prepared to go completely on my own to the U.K and pay a small fortune to fly business class, though it was a bit awkward when we left Chad in the economy section. That is one positive to waiting those extra few months, as Chad's own personal life also changed meaning he was able to join me. I have his bitch of an ex-girlfriend Charlie to thank for that. As expected it was Charlie who was responsible for the dumping. Chad keeps thinking over and over what he has done wrong, when the fact is he did nothing wrong at all, he was the best boyfriend she will ever have. It was her who was in the wrong, she put greed before love.

Chad first got the suspicion that something was up with her when she was acting weird at his 30th birthday party. She had left her mobile on the kitchen table and it was there that Chad saw several messages from 'Sausage Steve' that said how beautiful she was and when was she next going to come over. Chad, as any man would be, was rather suspicious of this and when he handed her phone back to her, he asked her who 'Sausage Steve' was. At the time she claimed the guy must have got the wrong number and that she would never cheat on Chad and that Chad was an untrusting boyfriend for going through her phone messages like that and how could he be so horrible to her by ruining the trust they had. Chad never touched the phone, the messages just pinged up on the screen, but still he felt really awful for what he clearly thought at the time was him jumping to conclusions and that it really was just a guy with a wrong number.

He thought nothing more of it until a few weeks later when he noticed Charlie was starting to wear different clothes to the usual shitty hippy harem pants she wears, and they didn't look like cheap clothes either. Maybe she just wanted a new image at work was Chad's first thought but he had a niggling feeling that something wasn't quite right, so he decided to go and surprise Charlie at her office with a bunch of flowers. When he got to her office, he finds Sausage Steve sticking his sausage in places he shouldn't. Now most blokes would go into a full-on rage and want to punch a guy's lights out if they saw they had been at it with their girlfriend but not Chad. He goes to the back of the office, pulls out a vase from one of the cupboards and puts the flowers in it, as he didn't want them to dehydrate, walks out calmly and says to Charlie, who at this point is trying to clamber back some dignity by scrambling around to find some clothes to put on, that it's over and she needs to collect her stuff, leave and never speak to him again. Unsurprisingly she didn't put up a fight, she took her stuff and went to live with Sausage Steve as apparently, he knows how to treat a lady, basically he buys her a whole load of expensive shit to keep her happy. That's not love, that's just a mutually beneficial relationship. He gets laid and in return she gets a Chanel handbag. I don't see that lasting long and I am glad that Chad saw the light and got rid of that hideous woman.

Chad found out afterwards that, 'Sausage Steve' is actually Steve Jones, owner of one of the biggest meat companies in New South Wales; 'Meat Madness'. Their offices were next door to Charlie's and that is how they ended up meeting. It seems kind of ironic that this swear down vegetarian would end up going with someone who spends all day butchering animals. Apparently, the vegetarianism was a phase she was going through to help her get through her relationship with Chad and she did actually love meat. I think what she really meant was if the price is high enough I will get rid of all my principles. Sausage Steve is no oil painting either, and being fifteen years older than Charlie I am really struggling to see what the two would have in common, other than him enjoying being someone's personal piggy bank.

That's another thing I loved about Ruby, she never once asked me about how much money I made or expected me to buy her random expensive crap as if she felt she was entitled to it.

The thought of Ruby slipping further and further away into the arms of another man is eating away at my insides. I am really hoping this letter idea Mum suggested does work. I mean she is a relationship therapist/psychologist/love guru after all. This is the first time I have fallen so deeply in love with someone and the letter really is the pouring out of my soul. The letter, secretly and securely placed in my backpack, must be version one hundred and fifty-one. Over the past six months I have changed it so many times, and over analysed every word trying to ensure I don't sound like a desperate whining twat. I want her to know that I am strong and I will care for her whatever life throws at us, and that I am willing to be committed to her and no one else. Sending this letter could be the worst or the best decision of my life but either way I need to give it to her to move forward with my life.

Now if mother would just hurry up and stop talking about menopausal sex, I can finally get on with my journey and send this letter to the girl I love and hopefully have sex with her, normal sex not menopausal sex she's only twenty-seven… oh god… now all I can think about is old people having sex. Why can't my mum talk about something normal for a sixty-year-old, like gardening or something, if she did maybe I wouldn't be so fucked up when it comes to relationships.

CHAPTER 3

I chuck the last of today's daffodils in the bucket ready to be thrown away. The end of an era and the beginning of a new one. It is weird to think in the space of ten months I have gone from not having a single iota as to what I want to do with my life, to running a market stall to now packing it in, in order to go and run my own floristry shop. That's not entirely true, I did have some idea as to what I wanted to do. I wanted to be an illustrator but with my emotions scattered into a million pieces leaving Australia, that wasn't meant to be. During that emotional time I had sketched and drawn so many pieces, so it wasn't that I didn't create any output, in fact some of the best drawings I have ever done came from those first few weeks I was back in England working out what I wanted to do in my life, but working in a different time zone caused problems trying to network and get people interested in my work as a new illustrator, and my one good connection; Charlie, well she seemed to be more interested in cementing her face to this guy called Steve than running her magazine anymore.

I stare in a daydream like state at the little yellow and red owl eyes that are gazing back at me. My favourite succulent. The Latin name for the plant is *Huernia zebrina*, which quite honestly sounds like a spell out of Harry Potter. I've been trying to learn all the Latin names of all the plants and flowers I stock as the older customers love trying to use all the Latin they have learnt from watching Monty Don on *Gardener's World* in order to outwit me. They seem to believe it makes them more sophisticated when in fact it makes them look like a pretentious twat. Although you can tell they get a kick out of it when I stare at them blankly and red-faced even if nine times out of ten it is because they have pronounced it incorrectly rather than me not knowing what the plant or flower is. Life is too short to worry about Latin or *vita brevior* if you really insist.

The *Huernia* is also known as a lifesaver, and there is some truth in that as this plant and many others have been responsible from saving me from a life of photocopying, drinking dreary cups of coffee sitting behind a desk and working for a belligerent boss. And for that I feel I owe the next chapter of my life to getting the best out of nature's beautiful gift of flowers and plants.

It was when I was meeting up with Lawrence for the first time in Loughton High Street that I saw the flower market stall for sale. The previous owner wanted to rent it out and retire to Benidorm, Spain, although by the orange tint of her skin you would've thought she had already been living there. The woman was the stereotype of Essex personified. Tracey was her name and she always had a full face of make-up, high heels and a mini dress on, whatever the weather. Yet despite her Barbie exterior, she was lovely and after a few cups of tea together she offered the market stall to me for a reasonable price for the year. Luckily, I had managed to put some savings away whilst I was in Australia, and it was just enough to cover the first six months of rent and my first purchase of stock. It was a risk but it was a risk worth taking as it was more successful than I could ever imagine. A few months later fate again offered a generous hand as just a few metres away from the stall a shop became vacant, and, with the inheritance from Granddad Shane, it was an opportunity too good to miss.

Despite forging a path in my motherland, I often think of Australia and the life I could have had with Ryan, my sister and her girlfriend Chloe if I stayed. I miss my sister Martha so much. As twins we will always have that invisible bond and that need to be together wherever each other is in the world. I really wish she was back home with me. And as much as I do not want to admit it, I miss Ryan too. I feel that there is a tie between us that I cannot cut.

I shouldn't have had that thought. That was a bad thought to have, nothing good will come of missing Ryan. It wasn't meant to be. Que sera sera and all that jazz. He isn't coming back and I've got too many good things happening in my life right now to be dwelling on the past.

I begin rolling up the tarpaulin on the stall ready for the next owner to take it over. Instead of flowers the new owner wants to sell pickled onions. Let's hope he doesn't get in a pickle about it all. And let's hope his business isn't as bad as my jokes. I continue to push the tarpaulin back, this is the worst part of the day due to the fact I need to jump up to reach the top of the stall to pull it fully down and it often takes a few attempts before I am successful, however this time I seem to have an assistant as I see a pair of hands grab the other side.

'Excuse me. What are you doing.' I say as sternly as possible trying to hide my shock and fear from this roving gloved hand.

'Oh, hey babe, sorry didn't mean to give you a fright. I just thought I would give you a hand,' he says as we push the tarpaulin the whole way back together.

It's Laurence. He looks different. Oh… It's his hair. What the… The blondeness is still the same but it looks like someone has put a bowl on his head and then cut round it with garden shears whilst drunk leaving the front shorter than the back. It is a complete mess.

'What happened to your hair Laurie?'

16

'Do you like it? You know I am a big fan of the mod scene and how everything looks so cool, sooo… erm… well I thought I might as well get myself a haircut like the mods, due to me buying something else, which I'll show you in a minute. The hairdresser said I looked just like Paul Weller,' he beams.

This hairdresser also needs to go to Specsavers, even Jay from *The Inbetweeners* has a better haircut than Laurence has right now. I can't tell him it looks bloody awful as I know he will get upset but I can't lie to him either.

'It's different. I'm sure I'll get used to it though. Anyway, what is this other thing?'

He looks guiltily back at me and I can sense trouble immediately. I rack my brain as to what else a mod could need other than a parka and a suit, neither of which Laurence is wearing. I just hope he hasn't blown his money on something stupid like a flea circus or some nail clippings from the cast of *Quadrophenia*.

'It's just down the road. I'll bring it over to show you.'

I watch him, both nervous and excited as he attempts a half walk half run down the road. He suddenly disappears behind a large black Range Rover and then re-appears wheeling a light blue scooter in my direction. What the shitting hell does he need one of those things for? Scooters are so bloody dangerous, a death-trap on wheels, especially around here and in central London. He has been mentioning for a while that he would like one, so it shouldn't have come as that much of a shock, although I didn't think he would actually do it, the haircut is one thing but this, I think he must have hit his head whilst at the hairdressers.

'So, this is it,' he says as he gently puffs in and out from the exertion of pushing the scooter towards me.

'It's a genuine 62 Lambretta TV175 Series 2. Seeing as

everything is going really well at work, and getting that promotion, I thought I would treat myself to it. I hope you don't mind.'

Well it's a bit late now. I can't really say no, it is his money and he has been exceptionally supportive in everything I am interested in and want to achieve. I take a deep breath and do my best to act grown up about this horrific thing on wheels.

'I will worry about you on that thing but I know you've wanted one for a while, so as long as you keep safe on it, you have my blessing.'

He lets out a huge grin, making him look more of an imbecile with that haircut, but it gives me a warm glow inside as I love to see him happy. He grabs me by the hand and whispers in my ear;

'There's also something else I want to show you.'

Jesus Christ, what else has he got to show me. I feel on the edge of a cardiac arrest already. It's almost like Laurence is going through a mid-life crisis at 29 rather than 49. He pulls me round to the back of the scooter and on the storage box at the back I see the words; 'The Lemon Tree – Florist delivery.'

'I thought I would offer a delivery service on Saturday whilst you are working, to help expand the business and to keep me busy on the weekend. Plus, it will be great to see what this baby will do,' he says patting the cream leather seat of the scooter.

I give Laurence a full kiss on the mouth to show my appreciation despite the fact something does not seem right about this. He's got the worst haircut of the year and is now riding something which is going to put me in a state of constant anxiety when he is on the road, but I know that he really does mean well and wants my business to bloom. Without him and his belief in me,

18

the Lemon Tree would be dead before it even came to fruition. These plant jokes really aren't getting any better, are they? As I try to feign interest in Laurence excitedly telling me all the details about where he found this 'mega awesome' scooter, I hear someone shouting my name.

'Oh Ruby. What's occurring.'

I could recognise that Welsh accent anywhere.

'ANDRE!!' I shout so loudly the whole high street stops and stares. I give everyone within sight a smile to show them it's okay he doesn't want to steal my purse, he is just a very good friend of mine.

'The one and only,' he replies.

I run over to him and give him such a tight and long squeeze, I feel I may have taken all the air out of his lungs. It is so good to see him, I haven't seen him in person since we sat and ate chocolate cake on the floor of my flat in Sydney almost a year ago. Time and life just got in the way of us meeting again sooner.

To prevent him suffocating any further, Laurence interrupts us and gives Andre a fist pump.

'Hey mate, how are you? Not still working in some sticky underground pub somewhere I hope.'

'Oh no Laurence, I've been making a bit of a name for myself as a poet and musician, you know, poems and songs about flying dragons and knights called Andre rescuing princesses from dangerous places. They say I am Cardiff's answer to Bob Dylan.'

'Well that sounds rather interesting,' says Laurence cautiously.

Andre chuckles that same child-like chuckle I remember him so fondly for.

'Nah not really, I've just been using my charm and wit to deal with unruly teenagers on behalf of South London social services, although I feel those traits are lost on those kids. I actually do poetry though but it's not exactly stadium sell-out stuff. I did a poetry gig last week in Camden about my Nan's cat to the biggest audience I have had yet. Three people. And two of those were the bar staff.'

'Well it all sounds much more interesting than a boring 9 to 5 job in an office,' I say encouragingly.

'Yeah well I won't be doing it for long as I am off to Canada in a few weeks. I could do with a change in scenery.'

'Canada! Oh, wow that certainly will be an adventure!'

A wry smile escapes on his lips; 'Oh you know me Ruby, I always like to have an adventure.'

It is then that I notice a woman standing next to him who appears to be just a couple of years younger than Andre, they are clearly related as they both have the same hazelnut eyes and round noses. Although the woman manages to carry off the features better than Andre, maybe it is due to her being a slightly bigger build than Andre who is basically a bean pole. Her dress sense is rather striking too, she is wearing a bright red cardigan with matching beaded bracelets and necklace and a 1950s style A-line red rose print dress. She is really quite something to look at and I can't quite believe I completely missed her when I started to speak to Andre. He must have realised I was staring as he decides to introduce her.

'Oh, in case you are wondering who this tag-along is. It's my sister. We were just in the area as it happens. I didn't realise you were so close to London. I always thought Essex was miles away

20

from here. Anyway, we are here as my sister is looking for a part-time job whilst she studies Fashion Design at the local University.'

'How come you never mentioned you had a sister before Andre?'

'Well she isn't as cool as me so I didn't feel the need to mention her to people.'

'Yeah right. More like you'd be cramping my style, I'm Catrina by the way.'

She pokes her hand between Andre and I. I like this girl she has some feist to her and if she is anything like Andre, we are going to get on like a house on fire.

'Nice to meet you Catrina.'

We firmly shake hands. I'm thinking she could work well in a role where she would have to deal with tricky customers and I'm thinking it's time to make a bold decision.

'Catrina, do you like flowers?'

'Oh, I adore them, I always try and incorporate them into my designs. The last skirt I made had a peony print.'

'Well Catrina this may be your lucky day as I am looking for an assistant in my new floristry shop, The Lemon Tree. I can't guarantee what hours yet, but you'll be making a huge difference to a new business.'

She stands there with her mouth wide open, before suddenly talking so fast in her Welsh accent that I begin to have trouble understanding what she is saying.

'Oh yes. It's a definite yes. That's so kind of you, I mean you haven't even met me before. Do you want to see my C.V? I mean you don't even know if I can work. I mean I can…'

'Take a breath Catrina. I don't need to see your C.V. the fact you have to put up with Andre as a brother is enough to show you are capable of working in a shop.'

We all laugh and Andre pulls a mock deeply offended expression.

'Over the next few weeks I'll need you to help me with setting the shop up ready for opening night.'

'All good with me. I'd be happy to get stuck in and make this the best florist shop in Essex.'

I had genuinely been looking for an assistant as running a shop is going to be more time consuming than the stall. Plus, I wanted to return the favour Tess gave me in Sydney to someone else. She gave me the opportunity to work at her shop despite the fact I was just a backpacker on a working holiday visa, and she knew nothing about me at all and worst of all I knew nothing about flowers. If it wasn't for Laurence taking me to see her, I probably wouldn't even consider floristry as a career now, and I certainly wouldn't be standing here offering a job at my own florist shop. I miss hanging out with Tess sometimes, we still send each other the odd postcard once in a while but I think she still feels bad about what happened to me on Bondi Beach, she felt she should have looked after me more. She's not to blame at all, it was me who decided to go with him to Bondi and it was me who could have said no, I'm just glad Ryan got there in time. I place my hand on my left arm where the scar is hiding under my long sleeved t-shirt and feel myself shiver.

'Right I think I need a glass of wine.' I say cheerily bringing myself back to reality and ready to enjoy the weekend ahead.

'Amen to that sister,' shouts Catrina, further cementing that it was the right decision to hire her to work for me.

'Give me a minute to pack this in the car and let's head off and celebrate new beginnings and the meeting of new and old friends.'

There are smiles all round and for the first time in a while life seems utterly perfect. Right now, no one can stand in my way of having the best life possible.

CHAPTER 4

'And that, ladies and gentleman, is how you become a successful cougar.'

Thank god she has finally stopped talking. The room erupts with applause at such a level you would have thought Steve Jobs had come out and shown everyone a new iPhone. I was always under the impression that those in academia were of the quiet sort but clearly not these guys. They are in love with my Mum's talk, okay it contained psychological terms and footnotes to academic articles, but essentially it was a DIY tool-kit on how to snag yourself a 'toy boy' or 'toy person' as my Mum tells me, you can't discriminate by gender, everyone apparently should find someone that helps them look 'youthful'.

I think Mum needs to look in the mirror as she has been looking pretty worn out in the past few months, due to her jetting around the world doing talks and basically being Larry's personal assistant, I swear a sloth does more work than that guy. According to Mum he needs all the assistance he can get as he has such a stressful job as an actor at the Opera House. All he does is prance about on stage, in the last performance he did, he didn't even have to speak. I mean of course, it is much more difficult than being an accountant and dealing with a client who hasn't paid all their bills in time, refuses to pay tax and allows their dog to piss all over the office whilst I tell them that what they are doing is illegal. I definitely think Larry has got the short straw, he clearly has the more stressful job.

Mum gracefully bows to the crowd and then it appears she wants to say something else, as she raises her hand to the audience. Obediently they pause in their adoration to hear what else she is about to preach. I swear these people need to be tested.

'Just one last thing… I would like to also thank my son Ryan and his friend Chad who are sitting just over there…' Mum points in my direction and I tried to slide down my seat to avoid being detected but Chad has other plans as he gives the crowd a wave and shouts 'G'day.' My cover and any respect I could have had in this room now blown.

'…and of course, my darling Larry who unfortunately couldn't be here today. Without you boys, I wouldn't be able to write such wonderful books.'

I need to start thinking of what I can do to upset Mum so she doesn't carry on writing these 'wonderful' books anymore, as they really are horrendous. Well horrendous for me anyway, everyone else seems to think she is the ultimate 'love guru'. Despite several people being desperate to see her as she walks off stage, I quickly rush over to her and grab her by the arm. We've only got thirty minutes before our train to London and I am determined we won't miss it. There is a letter in my rucksack that is burning to be sent and the sooner I get to London and on my way to deliver it, the better.

'Mum, don't forget we've got a train to catch in thirty minutes. We don't want to disappoint Uncle Terry, do we?' I say squeezing her arm a little tighter.

'Ah, about that Ryan, I've decided not to go. I've got a few people here I want to catch up with before I fly back tomorrow. Besides, I feel it would be too painful just to see your Uncle

Terry for just one day and then go again. I'll see him properly next year when I intend to be in London for a few months as a visiting professor. Send him my love when you see him. And don't worry, your Uncle will understand. Now go and catch that train as we don't want to leave him waiting, do we? See you both later.'

I let go of her arm, flabbergasted, I am not ready to say bye to her just yet, despite being a fully grown man. She then begins to turn away and smiles at her admiring followers who are all dying to talk to her. They are going to have to wait a little bit longer as I can't have my Mum just shrug me off like this. It's likely that we won't see each other for a whole year and despite her being the pinnacle of embarrassment sometimes, she is my Mother, and maybe, deep down, I am just a real big Mummy's boy who isn't ready to be on the complete other side of the world from her when I need her the most. I gently grab her shoulder to make her turn back to me.

'Mum. Before we both go, it would be nice to have a proper goodbye before we are separated for a whole year.'

She grabs hold of my hand on her shoulder and turns herself around and I see tears begin to form in the corner of her green eyes and the pitch of her voice go slightly higher as she speaks to me;

'You know I don't like goodbyes Ryan', she sighs heavily. 'I just want to pretend that you are on holiday for a bit and will return soon. It feels like I am losing my little boy forever otherwise.'

I feel her hand grip tightly on my long-sleeved t-shirt and just give a nod to show I understand. Now I understand why she wouldn't want to see Uncle Terry. She's right, goodbyes suck, and right at that moment I think of the terrible goodbye I had with Ruby.

She gives both Chad and I a kiss on the cheek followed by a warm embrace before going straight to the table with the wine and nibbles. I see her grab the glass with the largest amount of wine and take a large gulp before plastering a smile on her face to deal with her admirers swarming all around her again.

I hear myself say; 'I love you Mum. I'm going to miss you too, even though you are a little crazy sometimes'. Yet somehow the words never leave my lips, and on the outside I turn my sadness into a happy sort of face in order to show Chad that everything is going to be okay. There is no fooling Chad, he knows me long enough and well enough to know that I am just putting on a brave face and he places one of his buttery-popcorn hands on my shoulders to tell me he is there if I need him.

'Don't worry dude, London is going to be awesome. Besides from what your Mum says, your Uncle is a right laugh.'

'Yeah you're right Chad. London will be awesome but, in the meantime, can you take your hand off my t-shirt as I think you may be leaving a stain on it.'

'Oh shiiiitttt! Sorry dude! That popcorn was pretty tasty though. I'll get you a bag to make up for it. Actually, dude how about I put my hand on the other side of the t-shirt to even it out, it could look like it was meant to be a cool design or something?'

I just laugh in response, knowing that with Chad things can't stay miserable forever. We grab our rucksacks from the back of the room, I take one last look at mum who is now standing in the middle of the circle with all eyes on her. She is clearly in her element as her eyes are lit up and she is waving her arms around passionately as she discusses what she knows and loves best. We both catch each other's eyes and smile. She lifts her drink up towards me and I give her a mock salute before swinging my rucksack on to my shoulder and head towards the train station.

* * *

The train journey from Oxford to London was rather non-eventful, although there was a boy at the end of the carriage testing out a new whistle his grandmother had bought him for the journey meaning the rest of us had to have our music up full blast in our headphones to try to cover the noise. I can assure you hearing an added whistle to your music isn't like adding more cowbell to *'Don't Fear the Reaper'*, it is just bloody irritating. Why you would buy a small child a whistle I will never know, but interestingly his grandmother appeared to have hearing aids and I swear they were both switched off. Nevertheless, it was a nice enough journey and interesting to see some British countryside for the first time.

When we arrive at Paddington station, it's like entering a hive of bees, so many people heading towards us, behind us and even from the side, it's beginning to make me feel dizzy, Jason and the Argonauts probably had an easier journey than the one we are going to make to get to the tube station here. It doesn't help that both Chad and I have humungous rucksacks that several people keep walking into, almost knocking us to the floor.

After a few more knocks and laps around the main station we managed to locate the underground and then had the fun task of working out how on earth to get to Bethnal Green. The tube map looks like a kid has done a doodle with all the crayons in his colouring-in box, bloody frustrating and not helpful at all. After five minutes of scratching our heads and fending off the local tramp who wanted to know whether we knew where his pet squirrel had disappeared to, we finally work out we needed to get the yellow line to Liverpool Street and the red line to Bethnal Green. We hop on a train which we hope is going the right way as I struggle to know my left from my right most days, let alone whether we are eastbound or westbound, but thankfully it seems to be heading in the right direction. I struggle to see Chad throughout the whole journey from Paddington to

Liverpool Street as we are squashed down opposite ends of the train. I am standing next to or was pushed up against someone eating a whole bucket of fried chicken, whereas Chad appears to have the better end of the deal as he is squashed next to a petite lady with a huge rack on her that's right in his eyeline, giving him the best view of this whole journey.

Liverpool Street to Bethnal Green is a little bit better in that Chad and I are standing next to each other but again we're packed in like sardines, meaning I am up close and personal to Chad's armpit, which after all the travelling wasn't pleasant at all. Finally, we arrive at Bethnal Green, and thirty minutes later we are still trying to work out who and where Uncle Terry is.

In all the rush to get to England and to see Ruby, it never really crossed my mind to actually ask Mum what my Uncle looks like or to ask if she had any pictures of him. When I google his name it just comes up with adverts for terry towels, which I'm pretty sure is nothing to do with my Uncle. Other than Uncle Terry having a fear of flying, which is why we've never met before, and Mum thinking he is the biggest barrel of laughs in Britain, I know nothing else about him, which makes finding him in a busy underground station as easy as finding a needle in a haystack and even then at least you know what to look for.

Despite endlessly walking around and clearly looking lost, no one stops to help or ask if we require assistance. I thought Sydney was a pretty unfriendly place but here no one talks to anyone they all keep their heads down and walk determinedly to their destinations, avoiding all human contact. If you make eye contact with anyone, it feels like you are committing a criminal offence. I feel my stomach getting tighter, the sense of control, of believing I could do this, come to London and begin a new adventure, is quickly slipping away, to a point where I just want to chuck my rucksack on the floor and either scream or cry.

'Not having much luck are we mate?' says Chad as he runs his hands through his blond wavy hair, the sweat marks getting bigger underneath his arms.

'Doesn't look like it. Goddammit if only I had just asked her for a bloody picture or even a contact number…'

'Wait a minute… maybe that guy over there could be him.'

Chad points to one of the ticket machines on the left-hand side of the station where two men are standing, looking as if they are waiting for someone. The one on the left looks like the type of guy that buys those 'dodgy DVDs' underneath the counter, he is wearing a long camel coloured trench-coat despite being at most five foot two with a slight pot belly, just peeping out of the coat I can see a white shirt and grey suit trousers, neatly polished black brogues and dark black hair that, despite receding, has been slicked back to an inch of its life, whether the colour of his hair is natural is also debatable. I feel that he needs a black umbrella and briefcase to finish off the look. On the other hand, the guy next to him definitely looks like he could be my uncle. He is about my height, wearing grey jeans and a green t-shirt with a green army style coat and has that silver fox vibe going on. I'd like to think that would be me in about 25 years' time. Older but still looking good, he has to be my uncle.

We walk over, with Chad hovering behind me as I get closer, meaning I will have to make the first approach, which is fair enough as he is my uncle not Chad's. I take a deep breath and go in for the kill.

'Hi, I guess you must be my Uncle Terry,' I say stretching out my hand for him to shake it. Instead of the friendly greeting I expected back, he looks up from his phone, looks me up and down in disgust and hisses;

'Piss off you pervert.'

Well at least I can rule one man out of the hundreds of other men here in the hunt for Uncle Terry. The guy next to him in the trench coat suddenly pipes up;

'You must be Ryan?'

You cannot be serious, the one who looks dodgy with a capital 'D' knows my name, meaning he is probably my Uncle. Why God, why.

He sticks out his hand and gives a smile that makes him look less dubious and more like a small cuddly bear. I shake his hand back and confirm with him that he is actually Uncle Terry and not another crazy fan of my mother's who happens to know my name as well.

'I am indeed your Uncle Terry. I don't usually wear a suit but thought I would make the effort to greet my nephew and his friend. Normally I work at home, I do the accounts for a lot of the local theatre companies and so I have a wardrobe that consists mostly of...'

He pauses as if he has already said too much, but I am burning to know more about Uncle Terry, who he is as a person and what makes him tick, especially as he has just revealed he works in accounts, plus I will be living with this guy for a year so I need to see if we will all get along. Despite the looks, maybe he isn't so bad after all, from personal experience I know accountants are generally pretty awesome.

'This is Chad by the way.'

I point a thumb in Chad's direction and he appears as confused as I am that this guy could actually be my Uncle. Chad gives him a handshake, along with a restrained; 'pleased to meet you.' Chad's normal style of greeting people is a hearty slap on the back and a 'how are ya mate?' Chad is clearly still on edge.

'Apologies my mother couldn't make it.'

I really wish she was here right now though as it would make this whole meet and greet thing a lot less bloody awkward.

'Yes, your mother did send me a message to say she wouldn't be here. Looks like I will have to wait another year to see the wonderful Lara. I do miss her so...' he sighs, looks at the floor and begins to walk at a brisk pace.

It is almost as if he doesn't want to be associated with us in any way. I mean if anyone needs to be worried about their style being cramped, it is more likely to be me than Uncle Terry. He's dressed like Danny DeVito's weird brother for Christ's sake.

'Now boys, this is the first time I will have young men like you staying in my flat, so there are a few ground rules that I require you to follow. I ask that you do not challenge these rules and just accept them. If you do not like them then I suggest you find alternative accommodation. Understood?'

'Yes, Uncle Terry,' both Chad and I chime together as if we are back in school assembly. At this stage it is not like Chad and I have much choice on the accommodation front as Chad has yet to get a job and I start work next Monday, so I won't have the time to search for something else. Besides giving Ruby my letter is my main priority this weekend. Let's hope Uncle Terry's rules aren't too absurd. Although it wouldn't surprise me if he wanted us to hang upside down in a coffin during the day and to eat raw steak in the evening.

'The first rule is that there are to be no girls coming into this flat. I do not want my flat to be known as the local knocking shop. Secondly, there will be a curfew on the weekends. From 8pm to 2am you must either be out somewhere for this entire time period or in your room. You are not allowed to enter the flat or leave your room during this time. And thirdly, I ask that you

32

keep the flat tidy. This is not a hotel. I do not want to be picking up your stinky socks all across the flat. I have worked hard to have a nice flat, I do not want you boys ruining it. Other than that, you are free to do as you wish. Are you both okay with this?'

He stares directly at me, his brown eyes unwavering and looking to see if there is any sign of rebellion in them. Both Chad and I nod our head in agreement to his rules, knowing we have no other option but to agree. The second rule is rather weird but not unmanageable. I don't tend to be out on the town anymore anyway, I've got a girl to track down and I am sure once Uncle Terry feels more settled with us, he won't mind Ruby coming round, she's different to all the other girls out there anyway.

'That's all settled then.'

He smiles again and it leaves me confused. I'm pretty sure this is how serial killers reel you in to their lair. At first, they are nice to you, offer you the warmth of their home and use of their goods and then they chop you up and put you in a bin bag ready to be collected on Wednesday. I look at Chad to see if he is thinking along the same lines. He puts a mock gun to his head and shoots himself and I do my best to stifle a laugh.

Well living with Uncle Terry is certainly going to be interesting.

In order to keep the conversation going between us, I decide to ask him how to get to Epping Forest. I really hope it is nearby and I don't have to go on all the colours of the rainbow shown on the tube map to get there.

'It is quite straightforward, just get on an eastbound central line train stopping at Epping Forest. Why do you want to go there?'

'No particular reason. Just to see a friend of mine.'

For some reason I feel rather embarrassed talking about it with my Uncle Terry. There is nothing to be ashamed of, but saying anything to my uncle at the moment just feels awkward. And then, as if it could not get any more awkward, for just a moment Chad seems to have forgotten the need to be polite and restrained around my Uncle Terry and shouts;

'Yeah right mate. He's head over heels with this friend of his Tezza. He thinks it's the love of his life. Guy needs to stop being such a softie, don't you think Tezza?'

I see Uncle Terry squirm a little at the way he is being talked to. Right now, I think I would be more comfortable lying on a nail of beds than in the middle of a conversation with these two. However, Uncle Terry quickly regains his authority and makes us feel like we are naughty children again.

'Remember what I said Ryan. No girls allowed. And Chad, please do not call me Tezza. My name is Terry. You may be used to shortening everybody's name in Australia but not here.'

'Yes, Uncle Terry.' Christ, this is worse than being back at school. I am starting to wonder whether Mum was being sarcastic about him being a 'barrel of laughs' as this guy looks so wound up he makes a coiled spring look relaxed. A few moments of silence pass but it clearly gets too much for Chad. As much as I love the dude, he is not one to be a stickler for formalities but he is going to have to learn fast if we want to have a roof over our heads while in London, and yet as I think of ways for him to rein it in, he suddenly says;

'I think Tezza suits you. I'll call you Terry though as asked. I'm sure I'll get used to you and your dirty old man mac.'

Shoot. Me. Now. Uncle Terry's face has gone scarlet and he is breathing in and out slowly to calm himself down. I really hope he doesn't change his mind about us staying with him rent free, although I have a feeling that Uncle Terry had wished he added another rule to his list; if your name is Chad please do not speak in my presence.

The rest of the journey to Uncle Terry's flat is made in silence.

Despite the outside of Uncle Terry's flat looking like a typical industrial estate, the inside is complete luxury and looks much bigger inside than outside, which is a relief as every Aussie I know who's come over to London tends to end up living in a shoebox, or sharing a room with twelve others. Chad and I have a room each, Chad does have a sofa bed in the study but by the looks of things, it is the crème de la crème of sofa beds. It's even remote controlled so you can adjust the height of the bed and don't need to open it by hand. My bedroom has a double bed and even has a bathroom in it, and though I will need to share it with Chad, we really have scored well in getting such a nice place to live in the city.

After unpacking our bags and making ourselves at home in the flat, Uncle Terry makes us a curry to eat or Terry's Teriyaki as he seems to call it. It is like Uncle Terry has suddenly turned a switch from psychopath mode to friendly mode. I'm still not convinced he isn't a serial killer though so might keep my bed side light on tonight. Yet I feel more relaxed as we all have had a beer and generally talked about the work we do and for a brief moment everything feels normal and less awkward than the walk to the flat. I feel the sense of excitement for this adventure begin to creep up on me again and I relish the feeling. Yet after a few hours together and getting to know each other, things get weird again as he looks at his watch and notes that the time is now 8pm and we need to go to our rooms, obviously needing to find another victim to kill. Although I really hope there is a more innocent explanation to this curfew, maybe when I get to know him better I will ask him the reason why.

'Well you know what time it is boys,' he says sternly with his arms folded, showing he is not to be messed with when it comes to curfew time.

Chad rolls his eyes at me and thankfully Uncle Terry doesn't see but I agree with the sentiment. I think the last time I was sent to my room I was about seven years old and wanted to watch more *Teenage Mutant Ninja Turtles*. I didn't expect twenty-two years later to be told what time to go to bed again, I didn't even get to watch any turtles beforehand, however seeing as we are going to bed so bloody early I might see if it's on *Netflix* on my iPad. Thankfully I got the WiFi password from Uncle Terry earlier, although for some reason he has set his password as 'Queen TT'. We all say goodnight to each other and head to our rooms on cell block H. Okay this place is more like a palace than a prison but this curfew makes it feel like one.

This wasn't quite how I expected my journey in England to begin, although not unpleasant it has certainly been challenging dealing with a different way of life, a life less free than back home, a life now full of deranged uncles. However, it is the thought of Ruby that keeps me going on this journey and not heading straight back to Heathrow. I want to go and see her now but it's too late in the evening and what with Terry's stupid curfew rule it is best to stick to my original plan and see her on Sunday, there is more chance she will be in on a Sunday, a quiet day, a day I can hopefully speak to her on her own and give her my letter.

CHAPTER 5

Well Laurence and I have been 'dating', 'courting', 'seeing each other' or whatever you want to call it for nine months now, meaning things are pretty serious. According to my friend Floella, I can no longer put bananas in my basket upside down, I must now put them the right way up as I'm officially off the market. I never knew there was this whole banana code thing to explain your relationship status but maybe it explains why I was single for so many years.

On the topic of bananas, I think my parents are driving me to the brink of insanity. They have been pacing up and down all yesterday evening and this morning in anticipation of Laurence's arrival. The Duracell bunnies have nothing on these two. They have been asking me all sorts of irritating questions and getting into a frenzy. I know this is the first time that I have ever brought a boy to the house, well except for Si and Dave but they were family friends, so it is a bit different, and they are both so far down the weird spectrum that they were ruled out early on as potential son in law material. I mean Si used to openly pick his nose and eat it in front of my parents for Christ's sake. It shouldn't be a big deal, I say to myself with sweaty palms and a fast heartbeat.

Dad has rearranged the beer bottles in the fridge about ten times already, ensuring all the labels are at the exact same level and all facing the same way. Normally he doesn't care what the beer looks like as long as it is drinkable and within easy reach. He is only doing it as a way to look busy so Mum doesn't give him another task to do. The pair of them have been up since 5am chopping vegetables for today's lunch. With the amount of food, we have, we could feed a whole football team and still have spare. It is beyond ludicrous. She has even got out her best china for today, the set was a wedding present from my Mum's grandmother over 30 years ago. The last time this set got an airing was in 1986, several years before I was born when Mum was trying to show off to the new neighbours next door.

Unfortunately, one of our next-door neighbours wasn't quite as sophisticated as Mum and Dad hoped and earned himself the nickname 'Daredevil Derek'. 'Daredevil Derek' has a dog. A dog that lacks control and one that Derek insists he takes everywhere, even when told not to as fresh carpets had been laid. His dog walked around the whole of our house with muddy paws making our beige carpet brown and leaving Mum on the brink of a meltdown. 'Daredevil Derek' felt that as the designated 'Neighbourhood Watch' he should be entitled to a full tour of the house, just in case there was a masked intruder hiding under the bed. After the tour Mum then offered Derek some cake which he happily and greedily accepted before offering the few remaining crumbs on the plate to his dog. Due to the dog apparently having a tongue the size of a small rodent, he managed to lick the plate so hard it made Derek drop it on the floor and shatter into a million pieces, meaning Mum now has 21 plates of unnecessary dressy china instead of 22. She is also still waiting for an apology from Derek who seems quite oblivious to the chaos he caused. It is also the reason why the plates will only come out if royalty is arriving or someone particularly special, so let's hope for everyone's sake that Laurence doesn't have butter fingers.

Even though it is frosty outside, the windows are all steamed up, and it is feeling incredibly toasty in here due to all the food Mum has been cooking and the fact everyone is radiating stress for something that should be more of a pleasant experience; just four people enjoying a nice cooked meal. Well this is what I keep telling myself to keep calm, even though I have been wringing my hands for the last four hours.

I know when Mum is in a fluster as almost every other sentence is a question and she begins to imitate the road runner as she zips around the house. Last night she was using the hoover in one hand, a duster in the other to ensure the place was spotless. This woman makes Houdini look bad with the feats she does.

'So, it's been nine months since you've been together? Do you think now is the right time for him to see us? Is it early or late? I suppose nine months is enough time to bring a new life in the world. You're not pregnant, are you?' she says, as she sets a timer with one hand and begins kneading some dough on the other for the apple tart she is making, just in case there wasn't enough choice with the strawberries, chocolate forest gateaux and bread and butter pudding already laid out on the dining table.

'No Mum, I'm not pregnant, now quit with the questions will you, you're putting everybody on edge. Remember he is human just like you and me, so there is no need to start acting weird and putting your 'posh voice' on. It's bad enough that you are both dressed as if you are going to the races rather than an informal family gathering.'

'I don't put on a posh voice Ruby! That is the way I normally talk and yes okay, I am nervous but that is only because I want your boyfriend to like us poppet. I'd hate to give him the impression we weren't very nice or something.'

'Haha yes you do Sue. It's like Princess Anne has suddenly walked in the room;' interjects my Dad.

Great now he has really added fuel to the fire of stress that Mum is already engulfed in. I watch Mum's face go scarlet and see her clutch her throat as if to control her voice-box from betraying her again.

'Don't worry about it Mum.' I say trying to calm her down.

'I'm sure we will all get along fine and besides it should be Laurence who is impressing you, not the other way around.'

I am praying to the heavens above that he is on his best behaviour when he comes around as I am more concerned at this stage he won't live up to my parent's expectations, rather than him thinking they are on the road to Psychoville.

'Ding dong merrily on high…'

That's the doorbell, just in the nick of time too, before either Mum or I burst into tears at how ridiculous this is all turning out to be.

I am hoping he's out there and he hasn't already done a runner already due to that cringe-inducing doorbell Dad has had fitted. I head to the door, take a moment to pause as I view the silhouette in the stained glass door window take a gulp of air and pull down the front door handle…

CHAPTER 6

The softness of the pillows and the duvet I have cocooned around me makes it even harder to turn off the alarm I set for 10am this morning, thankfully it is a Sunday. I know what I need to do today, which is to walk straight to Ruby's house and tell her exactly how I feel. After thinking it over last night I probably won't tell her face to face, as I know I'll end up looking like a prat, instead I'll let the letter do all the talking so I can make a quick exit if need be, but hopefully this letter will show her how much she means to me. I mean it took me nearly a year to fucking write so something good should come from it. I feel myself begin to shiver and it isn't from the cold, I pull the duvet even further over my head but deep down I know I can't avoid this any longer if I want a shot at happiness. I need to get a grip and just do this.

As I slowly pull the duvet back down to face level, I begin to smell something cheesy, like the smell you get from sweaty socks. I wonder if Uncle Terry actually washed these sheets? As I begin to push the duvet down further, it is then that I see that I have a pair of feet right by my face, so close they are almost touching my nose. What the fuck? I must be in some sort of dream or that Teriyaki chicken Uncle Terry cooked contained some funky ingredients. I slowly pull myself up from my lying position so I can sit upright without waking this creature and find out what it is.

I peel back the duvet further to reveal the rest of the sleeping beast.

I breathe a huge sigh of relief as the rest of this creature's body is very familiar and if I wasn't in such a nervous state this morning, I would've given him a sharp boot in the side to get him out of my bed. Instead I decide to be nice as I do not want karma to bite me on the arse later.

'Chad what the hell are you doing in here?'

Chad makes a sort of muffled sound and turns over trying to grasp hold of some of the duvet that just seconds before had been snatched away from him. Eventually his grasping hand gives up and instead he lies on the front of his chest as if giving himself a hug. I try to gently shake his leg but still there is no sign of life. He is well and truly in dream land and I know from previous experience it is going to take more than just a few barks of his name and some hard shakes to get him back to the land of the living. I remember the year we went camping with school and there was a horrendous thunderstorm which caused tents to go flying up in the air along with all their contents, and if your tent wasn't in the air or being struck by lightning it was being flooded with water, it felt like the world was coming to an end, I of course kept my cool whilst the rest of the campsite were screaming like banshees. Chad, however, remained in his tent, blissfully unaware even when it begun to fill with water, as he continued to enjoy the world of slumber.

When he woke in the morning he thought one of the older boys had played a prank on him and made all his belongings wet whilst he was sleeping, not realising that an apocalypse was almost on its way that night, and then when he joined us at the campfire in the morning and saw us all wet and trying to dry our clothes, he changed his mind about it being the older boys making his tent wet and thought we had all gone swimming without him and the teacher made his clothes wet as a punishment for not getting up on time. It took Miss Perkins, our teacher, three attempts to explain the situation before he believed it.

I then suddenly remembered the secret of rousing Chad. This is not going to be pleasant. I crawl down the double bed to his face, lick my finger and stick it straight in his ear.

Chad immediately sits bolts upright as if he has had a taser fired right in his arse and begins to panic;

'Arghhh. Where am I? Who am I?... Dude what the hell are you doing in my room?'

'You're in my room bro. Your room is next door. The question is what are you doing in my room?'

He places his hand over his heart to control himself from the shock and takes a moment to breathe, blinks his eyes and then looks a few times at the door, then at me and then the bed and then suddenly it all begins to click in to place.

'Ah sorry Dude, I think I must've got confused as to what room I was in last night when I came out of the bathroom. What with it being dark and all the doors being the same...'

I see a slight tinge of pink spread across his cheeks, he is clearly embarrassed but we are friends and it is an easy mistake to make, especially as we are in a different country as well as a different house, so I try not to make it a big deal for him.

'No worries dude. I'm just glad it was you, not some weird yeti thing that snuck through my window.'

Despite me making light of the situation, he still doesn't make eye contact and tries to move the situation on.

'Right well now I am up, I might see if Tezza… oops I mean Terry… I don't think I will ever be able to get his name right… anyway, I am hoping he does an English breakfast, what with us being in the U.K and everything. I could murder some bacon. If not then those Rice Krispies at the top of the shelf have got my name written all over them.'

He heads out of my room but just as I think he has disappeared back to his own room, he pops his head back round the door.

'You're lucky I was wearing pants last night, normally I go commando.'

He winks and I throw a pillow towards the door, which he manages to close just before I could hit him square on. I hear him chuckle to himself on the other side, it doesn't take long for Chad to get back to his normal funny self.

A smile creeps up on my face. Even if things don't work out with Ruby, at least I know I will always have my best friend Chad. Then my heart begins to race again and I want to pull the duvet covers back over me but I resist. I get out of bed and perform a big stretch, the closest thing I will ever get to yoga. I head towards the desk in the corner where I have laid out my clothes for today, clothes I have agonised over the past few weeks, to ensure I will make the right impression when I see her for the first time in England. Next to the clothes is the letter that could make or break everything. I've gone over it so many times and had most of it checked by mother, bit of a weird thing to show your mother I know but she is a psychologist who specialises in relationships so it would be stupid not to, and also Chad who made sure I was honest but not soppy, girls don't like soppy as he found out with Charlie.

I put on each piece of clothing as carefully if they are made of tissue paper to ensure they remain in their pristine state; blue shirt, camel coloured chinos, brown leather belt and brown

44

brogues, all topped off with an Armani navy wool coat, a splurge in Sydney and well worth it with the cold weather. I hold off putting the coat on until I am out the door but make sure my hair is all in place and my teeth look clean before I head into the kitchen.

Chad is already sitting by the breakfast bar, looking as chilled out as always but this time, thankfully, he is wearing more than just his jocks.

'Good luck dude. I'm sure she will fall straight into your sexy man arms,' he says, as he eats a large mouthful of rice krispies, of which some have begun to cover the singlet he is wearing.

I thank him for his optimism and tell him that I will probably be back in a few hours. He gives me a mini salute in return, and I grab a banana from the fruit bowl for breakfast and force it down me, I really don't feel hungry due to my guts currently being in knots, but with all this adrenaline pumping through my body I need something to keep me going. It is then I see a potential opportunity for a present on the dining table; a bunch of lilies. I know she is a florist but it's the thought that counts right? I should have thought of a present to go with the letter but my mind was too busy freaking out about today to think of the details, I can give her the flowers now and make a joke, look cool and give her a better present later. Sorted. I think.

'Do you think Uncle Terry will need these?' I say to Chad as I take them out of the vase and let the water from the stems run off.

'Nah mate. He hasn't yet noticed that I polished off the last of the Chardonnay in my room last night that I smuggled out of the fridge so you'll be fine,' he says, picking the rice krispies off his vest and popping them straight back into his mouth.

I give the lilies a final shake over the sink, put my coat on and then head out the door ready to embark on a journey that could just change my future.

***

Somehow by a miracle and *Google Maps*, I arrive right outside Ruby's house. Well I hope it's her house and her sister didn't give me a fake address and instead has sent me to some Essex gangster's house or something in revenge, although that would be karma for permanently borrowing those lilies. My whole body feels like it doesn't belong to me right now and the thumping in my ears is getting louder and faster. I want to run away but if I do I know I will never find the answers I am looking for.

'Ding Dong merrily on high…'

Well that's an interesting doorbell, probably a bit early for Christmas considering it is only February but still, welcoming enough. As I squint desperately through the stained glass windows in the door I can make out three figures, it looks like two are holding back by the staircase while one, female in shape walks towards the door. I begin to jog on the spot to burn off my nerves and because its bloody freezing, I don't think I will ever get used to the cold, harsh British weather.

Please be Ruby, please be Ruby. I don't want to be castrated by some psychotic female skinhead in her basement, I'm too pretty for that type of thing, plus the accounting world need a genius like me, oh who am I kidding I'm going to be dog meat for the local Rottweilers. Well planet earth it was nice while it lasted.

I hear the locks rattle and a voice saying 'just a minute', as the door slowly opens I feel on the verge of passing out as inch by inch the door reveals more of Ruby's beautiful body until we are both standing opposite each other, her eyes light up immediately.

'Hey… oh my god… what the…'

Before I get to make any sort of response, two other faces make an appearance at the door.

'Come on in Laurence, it is so nice to meet you,' says the first face, a slim woman who has the same thin nose and plump lips as Ruby but slightly more wrinkled skin than her and straight grey medium length hair. I am going to take an educated guess that this is Ruby's mother.

'Err I'm not La…'

Before I can explain who I am the second face steps in front of Ruby and gestures for me to enter. Again, I am going to guess this is Ruby's dad: he has a mass of blonde curls that are starting to go a yellow colour, you know that colour blonde hair goes right before it turns grey, a rosy cheeked face and a figure best associated with the sport of darts rather than the sport of athletics.

'No need to have a conversation at the door mate, come on in. Sue has put on a roast dinner for lunch and you can't eat it out there. I'm presuming these are for Sue as well…'

He snatches the bunch of flowers from my hand and gives the bunch to Sue who responds with a thanks as if I had given her a thousand pounds rather than just a second-hand bunch of flowers.

Ruby's dad's accent is familiar; he is an Aussie just like me. She never told me he was an Aussie, in fact I don't know as much about Ruby as I should. As a man in love with her, I should have asked her questions about her background rather than me telling her about me and my psychologist Mother who has a penchant for toy boys, but she was such a good listener and when she looked at me with those blue eyes it was hard not to stop.

The fact that her dad is an Aussie could work to my advantage today though. I step into the house, brushing past Ruby, who is beginning to look confused and frustrated simultaneously. The small contact I have with her makes the hair on the back of my neck stand on end.

'Mum, Dad that isn't…'

'Look stop causing a fuss Ruby, let's get this nice young man settled with a nice drink and we can deal with whatever is playing on your mind later…' says Ruby's mother.

Like a petulant toddler, Ruby crosses her arms in frustration as she looks at me angrily and all I can do in return is shrug my shoulders before I am ushered into the living room by Sue, still clutching the flowers tightly in her right hand, the flowers that should have gone to Ruby, oh well that will teach me for taking them from Uncle Terry anyway.

'You have a lovely home Mrs. Samuels.'

'Why that's very kind of you to say.'

'No, I mean it I can see you have made some clever colour choices, it really helps maximise the light you have coming in from the front windows.'

I see her blush a deep crimson colour from the compliment. If I haven't got the dad on my side I can definitely say that I am beginning to get Ruby's mum on my side.

Women love a compliment and I am happy to give them to them if I know I can get something in return.

'Right well I better put these flowers in a vase, otherwise they'll be dying of thirst. Oh, I don't think we have properly introduced ourselves have we Dave? I think we got so excited that Ruby has brought a boy home for the first time that we completely forgot. How rude of us.'

'Well now you know I'm Dave, Ruby's dad. In my youth I was a pretty good rugby player, very good at tackling other players and taking them down, even got the nickname 'Dangerous Dave'. Hopefully I won't ever have to tackle anyone again though, I'm getting too old for that kind of shit…' he says to me directly, looking into my eyes.

That was certainly a subtle way of saying if you mess with my daughter, you are dead. I think it is time I tell the truth before I get myself into any further trouble, although Ruby seems to have a bit of a smile on her face, despite trying to pretend she is still annoyed with me.

Sue then decides to go back into to the kitchen as she thinks she can smell burning, leaving me and Dave locked in eye to eye combat. I have a feeling that if I don't come clean now, Dave really is going to be using his tackling skills again.

'And I am actually…'

'We know who you are mate, you're Ruby's boyfriend, no introduction needed,' Dave says as he gives me a hearty pat on the back.

If only that was true.

'Right I better get you a drink mate. I presume you won't say no to a beer?'

'A beer would be great but I just need to clear something up…'

'Ruby, get the boy and me a beer will ya. There's some at the bottom of the fridge.'

Ruby stands there open mouthed at the request. Neither her or I can believe what is happening.

'You know where the fridge is don't you love?' he says not clocking why his daughter is behaving so weirdly around me considering I am meant to be her 'boyfriend.'

Ruby doesn't respond to her dad but just raises her hands towards her head, as clueless as I as to how to deal with the situation I have found myself in.

'Take a seat boy and take your shoes off, you're not part of the furniture so make yourself at home.'

Like an obedient dog I sit straight down and Dave does the same and I try to think of a way to reveal my true identity.

'DING DONG MERRILY ON HIGH…'

'Oh Dave, I really wish you would change the ringer for the door, Sue shouts from the kitchen… just a simple ring will do, it can be rather embarrassing having that as a door bell…'

'I like it, it gives off a kind of festive vibe,' he says knowing full well he won't change it. He clearly is a man who likes to have a laugh and wind people up. In fact, he reminds me a little bit of me, albeit in personality not looks, he is certainly older and rounder around the middle than I am.

'Well I guess I better stop what I am doing in the kitchen and go off and find out who it is…' says Sue as she pops her head round the living room door still wearing her apron and oven gloves.

'Ta Sue, you're a doll.'

'And you're a lazy fat lump,' she responds rolling her eyes.

They both chuckle and then Dave swings round on the sofa so we are again eye to eye and I can feel my knees begin to knock against Dave's.

'So, from your accent mate, it sounds like you are an Aussie too,' he says as he takes the beer from Ruby who has now reappeared and gives me a softer and more genuine smile than before as she sits on the edge of the sofa opposite. It looks like her anger towards me seems to have dampened a little.

'Born and bred,' I reply as I take a swig from my beer, thankful that I can finally answer something truthfully.

'You'll have seen the atrocious behaviour in the cricket recently. Those boys have really made a fool of us Aussies.'

'Yeah, I can't believe they would do something so stupid. That's not the Aussie way of doing sport.'

'Exactly. Blokes at work have been giving me shit. I've been finding sandpaper between all my files at work this week.'

I laugh and feel that maybe now is the time to come clean as to who I really am. I like Dave and Sue and I also do not want another reason for Ruby to be upset with me.

In the background there seems to be some sort of commotion going on and I hear Sue call out Ruby's name from the front door.

'RUBY… RUBY… can you come here please, this man outside is claiming to be your boyfriend.'

I look towards Ruby and see a lightning sharp change of face, from staring at me and her dad in a dream-like state, to the look of a startled deer.

'Coming Mum. Ryan you better explain yourself to Dad.' And with that bombshell she darts out of the room to the front door.

'RYAN. I thought your name was Laurence.'

Fuck. Let's hope he really doesn't want to try out rugby tackling me to the floor. I quickly stand to attention ready to leg it at a moment's notice.

'Sorry Mr Samuels, I have been trying to tell you that my name is Ryan but I just couldn't seem to get a word in edgeways. I am just a friend of Ruby and Martha's, we met in Australia. I've just moved to London so thought I would say hello and see how she's doing.'

I screw both of my fists up into a tight ball awaiting either the verbal or physical attack or both from Dave to be unleashed, for an extra measure I also screw my eyes up and click my feet together. This is how Dorothy got back to Oz wasn't it, so maybe it could work for me, although at the moment I just appear to be getting carpet burn on my feet.

A boom of laughter fills the room and I slowly open one eye and I see Dave nearly on the floor almost crying his eyes out with laughter. His response is so infectious that it makes my shoulders bounce up and down, and I join in laughing at how ludicrous this whole situation is.

He suddenly composes himself and I decide to reign in my laughter as well in case there is a sting to this merry amusement of his.

'I thought you were too good to be true,' he says as he pats me on the back.

'You have certainly given me a story to tell the grandchildren one day. It will also teach us for being so bloody in ya face like that. No need to go back to formalities mate, you can still call me Dave even if you aren't Ruby's boyfriend. Good to chat to another Aussie actually. Sometimes miss the ol' country and get a bit sick surrounded by Pommies all the bloody time. Sit back down mate, there's always room for one more at our house.'

I reluctantly sit back down as part of me wonders whether I really do want to be here and see Ruby with her boyfriend here. I feel awkward and also extremely jealous, especially as her parents are so nice and so normal in comparison to mine.

I hear Sue's voice as she calls Ruby's dad.

'Dave… Dave… I think there has been a bit of a mix up.'

Sue comes back through the living room door with Ruby and a guy who I presume is Laurence standing behind her. I knew through Martha on social media that Ruby now had a boyfriend but I didn't plan to meet the guy in person, in fact I don't want anything to do with him. The impression I got from Martha was that he wasn't anything serious, although she did tell me to leave them alone as I shouldn't interfere with fate, what is meant to be will be. That's easy for her to say, she didn't have a bitch called Tanya fuck up her intended fate with Ruby. I thought he would be an easy obstacle to remove once I had told Ruby how I felt, but I have a feeling it will be more difficult than I envisaged. I want to punch the guy in the face but instead I sit there grinning on the sofa like a well-trained monkey.

'Don't worry Sue. The boy has told me everything. He is just a friend of Ruby and Martha's from Aus. Teach us for being so forward won't it Sue. I said he might as well stay though.'

'Oh, we are silly aren't we Dave? Don't worry Ryan, the more the merrier. There should hopefully be enough food for all of us.'

'So, you are Laurence, I presume?' Dave says as he goes over to shake the guy's hand.

As he does so I take a long hard look at what I am up against, and to be quite honest he isn't at all who I thought Ruby's boyfriend would be.

Firstly, what the fuck is up with his hair. It looks like he volunteered to be a model for the blind hairdresser's association. The front is all short, with the back being longer almost like a mullet and I am pretty sure the bright blond streaks running through his dark blond hair aren't natural. Other than his bogan Barry haircut, he seems to be of a good build, both he and I would probably be equal in a fight as we're about the same weight and height. He also appears to be one of those annoying people who, whatever the situation; weddings, funerals, death and destruction, he would be smiling just out of habit.

'Well I've just told Ryan here, that I was a pretty good rugby player back in the day. And I don't like to carrying on practicing if you get my drift Laurence.'

Laurence just stands there grinning, and holding Ruby even closer to him as if using her as a barrier against her dad. I settle further into the sofa and take another swig of my beer, it looks like things might be getting interesting.

'What happened to your hair mate? Did someone use their garden shears on your head?'

I am glad I'm not the only one who thinks this guy's haircut is idiotic.

'I got it cut last week. I'm a big Paul Weller fan and love the mod look. I've always wanted to have my hair the same as him and seeing as I now own a Lambretta scooter, it seemed like the best time to get it cut.'

'Oh right. If I were you I'd ask for a refund. Although if I ever can't find a mop for my floors, I'll know who to call for a replacement.'

He gives me a wink knowing he is going to have great pleasure winding up Laurence with his hair, and to be honest the guy is asking for it.

'Daaaaad,' wails Ruby.

'David. Don't be so mean. It's an unusual cut, clearly must be the trend for young people nowadays.'

Even I know that's Mum speak for 'what the fuck is that haircut.'

'Sorry Laurence, I tend to wind people up. You'll just have to get used to it. Ruby grab the man a beer and we can all sit and watch the rest of the rugby together. It's Ireland versus Japan so should be an interesting one. Do you like rugby Laurence?'

'Well I'm actually more of a football fan. I don't know much about rugby.'

'What team do you support?' asks Dave.

'West Ham.'

'Christ. He gets worse,' whispers Dave to me, although I'm pretty sure Laurence heard. I do my best to keep a poker face.

'Well there is nothing wrong in learning about a new sport, especially one as majestic as rugby. Take a seat and be ready to be enthralled by one of the best games on the planet.'

Ruby returns with a beer and then disappears into the kitchen to help her Mum with lunch and we take our positions to watch the game. Dave and I sharing one sofa and Laurence perched awkwardly at the end of the armchair trying to feign interest. It is pretty clear this guy doesn't know the difference between a try and a touchdown but top marks for attempting to get on the old man's side by trying to get involved.

To Laurence's relief, after what must have been an agonising thirty minutes for him, Sue calls us through to the dining room for lunch.

And my god, she wasn't joking when she said there would be enough food for all of us, it looks like she has cooked enough to feed a small army.

'Sue, it looks delicious. Thank you. I can't wait to tuck in.'

'Thank you, Ryan, it is always a pleasure to have an extra guest round, especially when they are as polite as you.'

Laurence realises that he better suck up to Mrs Samuels as well to earn some Mum points, but somehow misses the mark.

'Mrs Samuels, this looks wicked,' Laurence says as he nabs a piece of broccoli off one of the trays and plonks it straight in to his mouth.

Now I'm glad I am here with Laurence. He is making me look great with all these schoolboy errors he is committing. Probably down to nerves but still, even I know you need to thank your host and wait for the call to get your plates and begin eating, and I am an Aussie.

'Yes, please do help yourselves,' Sue responds and thrusts a plate into Laurence's hand.

He takes it, still grinning, oblivious of the faux pas he has committed. If there was a grade in impressing a girl's mum I'm pretty sure I would be getting an A and Laurence a D.

I take a plate from Sue and again thank her, knowing that British people love to thank everyone even when they aren't being nice. I head straight to the meat section of the table and place a couple of slices of ham and roast chicken on my plate ensuring I have enough to fill my stomach but not too much that I give Sue and Dave the impression that I think I am at an all you can eat buffet.

'The sign of a true Aussie there, always going for the meats first,' says Dave as he places another chicken wing on his already stacked plate of food.

'Are you going to have any chicken Laurence?' says Sue in attempt to get Laurence involved with us boys.

'Oh no Mrs Samuels, I am a vegetarian. I have been since I was 12.'

'You can eat chicken, though can't you? Everyone likes chicken surely.'

'Mum. I told you before that Laurence is a vegetarian. Of course, he can't eat bloody chicken. A chicken is an animal. Vegetarians don't eat animals.'

Wow. Ruby is in a bit of a feisty mood this afternoon, although I have a feeling that both Laurence and I may be responsible for her attitude.

'Sorry Laurence, it completely slipped my mind. I can be a bit of a dippy cow sometimes.'

'It's okay Sue… erm Mrs Samuels, the vegetables and Yorkshire puddings will ensure I won't go hungry.'

His plate is already the broccoli equivalent of the leaning tower of Pisa. I doubt he will go hungry either.

Sue begins to blush with embarrassment at the situation, and fusses over the food, muttering she wished she'd cooked a nut roast. I feel that I need to do something to rescue the situation before it turns into a full blown 'vegetarian-gate' situation.

'Well that's good news Sue as it means all the more for me,' I say as I grab some more chicken on my plate to really emphasise the point home.

'Not if I get there first' says Dave as he steals a chicken wing off my plate, and we all begin to laugh.

***

The rest of the lunch goes smoothly and despite the first couple of hiccups with Laurence it appears they warm to him a bit more, although I still don't like him. Mind you, even if he was an exact replica of Chad I still wouldn't like him.

The conversation naturally peters out and I decide it is best for me to make a move as Chad is probably wondering where the hell I have got to, and I feel I should end on a high before I end up committing any faux pas in front of Mr and Mrs. Samuels.

'Right, I think it is time I make a move back to my Uncle Terry's. Thanks Sue and Dave for your excellent hospitality and lunch. It was great to meet you both.'

'You're more than welcome son. If you ever need a hand with anything whilst in London or are passing this way again be sure to drop in,' says Dave as he gives me a hearty slap on the back, so hearty I have to hold on to the table to prevent me falling into it.

'I ditto that Dave. It is lovely to see that Ruby has such nice friends.'

I feel my throat get dry and tight. I think I am still suffering from jet lag, Ruby's parents are so generous and kind. Just a few hours they were strangers and now they feel like friends, in fact they are the parents I wish I had, rather than a father who thinks he's still twenty and a mother who is a crazy psychologist.

'I will show you the way out Ryan, it was so good to see you', says Ruby as she gives me a small squeeze of my arm, further inflating my sense of hope that something could work out between us, instead of her and that blond bimbo at the dinner table.

As we get to the hallway, it is just Ruby and I on our own, I need to act now as this will be my only chance to give her the letter in private.

'Apologies for the mix up earlier and the fact my parents are super embarrassing. I'm sure you're not used to such silliness what with your Mum's celebrity status and things…' she says as she circles the carpet with her left foot, evading eye contact.

'I think your parents are cool. In fact, I wish they were my parents. And I need to apologise for turning up like this and causing this situation to begin with.'

'Oh really,' she says, shocked at my approval of her parents. 'I'm so glad you like them… I have a feeling they may like you more than Laurence. Dad certainly took a shine to you.'

I feel a warm feeling in my stomach, even Ruby noticed that her parents liked me. There is no time to lose now, I need to give it to her.

'Before I go Ruby, this is for you.'

I hand her the letter I have been pinning all my hope on since the day she left, my hands shaking.

'I am hoping it will give an explanation for my behaviour and my feelings for you and if you want to… you want to… maybe start over… that we could be friends or something… actually it's probably best you read the letter and come to your own decision.'

We look at each other straight in the eyes, both wanting to say more out loud than we should. Blue on green. Those blue eyes are deeper than the ocean. I desperately want to hold her, feel her skin on my skin, we are standing so close, in touching distance. I feel a spark between us like I did when we were together in Sydney and I wonder whether she feels the same. Yet just at that precious moment, Laurence comes along and drapes his arm over Ruby to make it clear this girl is still his… for now.

'What have you got there Ruby?'

'Oh nothing, just a letter from my sister Martha that she asked Ryan to hand deliver as a surprise. It will be weird twin and girly stuff so you won't want to read it,' she says as she stuffs the letter into the back pocket of her jeans and out of Laurence's prying eyes.

'Okay cool' he responds. It is clear from his demeanour that this encounter with me is anything but cool. We won't be friends but I don't care, he is just an inconvenience I am happy to remove so Ruby and I can be together.

'Well Ryan I guess you must be off then?' he says as he tightens his grip around Ruby.

I take that as my definite cue to go. In my head I was hoping for a more romantic encounter where Ruby would be bowled over by my thoughtful letter and we would have a heart to heart and instantly go back to how things were, the two of us, a perfect couple.

I quickly slip my shoes and coat on and make my way out the front door, shouting my goodbyes to Ruby's parents and giving a firm handshake to Laurence to show I'm not someone who can be easily pushed over. I then warmly embrace Ruby for as long as is socially acceptable drinking in the smell and feel of her in the few seconds we are connected.

As the door closes behind me, I turn and whisper 'I love you Ruby' and then make my way back to Bethnal Green with a feeling of hope and trepidation, knowing that the most vulnerable part of me is spilled onto a few pages that are finally in Ruby's possession. I just hope it wins her back.

CHAPTER 7

'I think that went pretty well don't you Rubes?'

'Haha very funny Laurence.'

'What's so funny? I thought it all went well, everyone got along.'

He looks at me completely seriously and all I want to do is scream and let down the tyres of that stupid moped of his. How could he honestly think that tonight went well? He turned up late, looked like he had gone through a hedge backwards, and managed to make a simple conversation between a group of pleasant grown-up adults look excruciatingly difficult. I am pretty sure I wasn't like that with his Mum and her partner. I turned up on time, made sure I looked neat and engaged in small talk, which included feigning an interest in his mother's ingrowing toenail on her right foot. I almost brought up the carrot cake she gave me when she was describing how they remove it, yet I remained composed and vomit-free the entire meeting.

His mother also kept asking whether she needed to buy a hat soon for a special occasion. Wink wink. Nudge nudge. Considering how her first marriage went, I'm not sure she is really the best person to encourage people to walk down the aisle after just a few months of dating, but it certainly showed she liked me enough to encourage her son to marry me. I haven't met his dad yet but maybe beforehand I should get myself a poodle perm, arrive on a tandem and do the splits in a bright green leotard in the dining room, just to show I really am the girl for Laurence. I know I'm new to this whole 'meet the parents' thing but I'm pretty sure the way Laurence behaved isn't the way you should behave in front of people's parents. The way Ryan behaved made him look like he was my boyfriend. not Laurence. I think I will have to have a conversation with Laurence at a later date to get his act together, but in order to keep the peace between us I will let it slide for now.

'Err yeah I guess it went okay Laurence… anyway have a good night and text me when you are back so I know you get back okay.' We exchange a peck on the cheek, knowing that we probably have an audience behind us which forbids us from engaging in a proper kiss.

Before he puts the key in the ignition, he looks up at me and says;

'Ah, just before I head off, one more thing – that Aussie fella… erm what's his name. I think it might have been Rory?'

'You mean Ryan.'

'Yeah. What's the deal with that guy?'

'Oh, he is nothing to worry about, he is just an old friend of mine from Australia. He probably just wanted to catch up with friends now that he is living in London.'

'He seems like a nice guy, next time you hear from him, tell him I said Hi too.'

Finally he puts the key in the ignition and then places his helmet over his head, it is one of those god awful helmets where the face is fully exposed making him look like Wallace from *Wallace & Gromit* rather than a sexy rugged biker, and then, after a few attempts at bringing the small hairdryer of an engine to life, he waves once more and slowly trundles off into the distance.

That is the first time I have seen Laurence act so passive aggressive over a man I might be friends with. When I chat to Andre, he barely blinks an eyelid, but with Ryan, something has irked him. Maybe he could tell I was lying and that we were more than just friends during my time in Australia, especially as I never mentioned to Laurence in our texts that I was dating someone, and the fact that Ryan was the one who saved me from dying on Bondi beach. I don't like to talk about that incident, Laurence asked me about the scar once but I quickly shut it down. It was none of his business then and I don't intend to make it his business now.

As I turn to go back inside, I see 'Daredevil Derek' pretending to fix his net curtains, he and I both know he was having a full look at the comings and goings of 32 Greenacre House. He even has a pair of binoculars around his neck, which I am pretty sure you don't need when trying to repair net curtains.

I give him a wave to show I have seen him and he's been caught red handed spying. He gives me a sheepish wave back and I see that his cheeks have gone bright red, serves him right for staring. Just before I open the front door, I feel my cheeks go a similar colour as Mum and Dad are standing in our front window blowing kisses in my direction and pretending to embrace each other passionately. I roll my eyes at them and all this seems to do is encourage them more. God they can be bloody embarrassing at times, thank god neither Ryan or Laurence were here long enough to see what nutcases these two really are, although how they managed to mistake Ryan for my boyfriend for so long this afternoon I will never know.

As I come back into the living room, my parents are grinning wider than a Cheshire cat knowing that they have scored ten out of ten on the embarrassment scale due to the colour of my face.

'You don't think we could spend the whole day being serious, do you?' says Mum half-giggling as Dad stands in front of her and begins pulling one of his big gurns, a trait that fortunately my sister inherited and likes to use, and one I am glad missed my gene pool.

'You do know your face will get stuck like that.' I say to Dad.

'Oh, don't be such a misery guts Ruby, we are just having some fun. That Ryan is a great laugh, he was cracking more jokes than I did when we were watching the rugby together. Great bloke.'

'I agree David, Ryan is a lovely young man. Very chatty and engaging.'

Well I am glad they like Ryan but what I really want to know is what their thoughts are on Laurence. Maybe I am overreacting and they didn't find his behaviour as bizarre as I did.

'And Laurence? Did you like him?'

Mum can tell that I am looking for some approval of Laurence so gives her tactful Mum answer of 'I'm not sure about this man but I'll say something which I think will pacify my daughter in case she goes crazy'.

'Interesting fellow and interesting choice of hairstyle.'

'Haha you can say that again Sue, the mullet was one of the reasons I decided to leave Australia in the 80s but I see that it is still alive and kicking here too.'

Mum tries to stifle a laugh and I just want the ground to swallow me up whole. Just when I think everything might work out with

Laurence, Ryan comes along and throws a spanner in the works. The one who shouldn't be right manages to win over my parents and the one that is my Prince Charming forgot to use his charm and any ounce of common sense he may have. Seriously, even Shrek would've done a better job than he did impressing my parents.

'Well to be honest I can't explain the haircut but as to his behaviour I think he was just a bit nervous that's all. He isn't normally like that.'

Mum can see that I am on the edge of a breakdown from this evening and puts her arm round me.

'Don't worry love, I am sure we were all a bit nervous today and I'm sure we will get to know him in due course. The most important thing is that he likes you and will look after you.'

'And if he doesn't I'm sure that your friend Ryan will be happy to step into his shoes. Just make sure he doesn't go all mullet mad on you like the other one.'

So much for him being the protective dad and not wanting his daughter to fraternise with the opposite sex, it seems that instead he is happy for me to go out with any guy as long as he doesn't look like something out of an 80s music video. Part of me wants to go full Annie Lennox on my dad and have short cropped ginger hair and see how much joke cracking he will do then. Actually, knowing my dad, he would probably need to be hospitalised for laughing so hard.

'David that's enough now. Ruby has had an emotional day,' she says as she rubs my right arm up and down.

'Sorry Ruby I don't mean to upset ya. Carrying on the 80s theme though I think we should all get a Pina Colada freshly served by yours truly. I think we deserve one after all the fun we've had

66

today,' says Dad as he begins to rub his hands together.

Mum nods enthusiastically and heads towards Dad who slips his hand round her waist as they do a conga towards the kitchen and shout;

'We all want a pina colada… la la la la la…'

I let out a sigh of despair and just like a mopey teenager, I mumble that I am heading to my bedroom, my heart beating faster each step I take as I know that other than feeling sorry for myself, I have a letter in my back pocket from Ryan that I desperately want to read.

A letter that he was going to post but thought was better to give in person. A letter my sister knew was coming but for some reason forgot to tell me that she had given Ryan my address. It doesn't make sense and why after all this time does he want to see me and what is so important in that letter that he can't tell me to my face. So many months have gone by without contact, I thought he would have moved on with a tart like Tanya by now. Well there is only way to find out what he wants and that is to open and read this letter…

CHAPTER 8

I cannot wait to fill Chad in with one of the weirdest afternoons I have had in a long time. In fact, this afternoon has been a lot more fun than some of the dates I have been on over the past few years. Just when I thought Ruby couldn't be any more of an awesome chick, she's also got some awesome parents. Her dad and I had a great chat about cricket and beer and just general bloke stuff and her Mum is an absolute delight who laughed at all my jokes.

It was hilarious that they genuinely thought I was Ruby's boyfriend when I turned up and to be honest, I probably could've pulled it off if Laurence hadn't turn up. If he really liked Ruby, he would've arrived on time. He better not cause her any issues other than embarrassment as he will have me to answer to. I might not like the guy but I don't want to see Ruby get hurt, she has suffered enough pain already, flashing back to that scene on Bondi beach brings back memories I just wish I could forget forever.

I feel rather smug at the moment as I think I might have upstaged Laurence, I swear I could see a look of disappointment in her parents' eyes when they realised Laurence was a bit more than the local door to door salesman, mind you with the look he was rocking he'd be a perfect candidate for the 1980's double glazing industry.

I think I even managed to get her dad's seal of approval, a pretty tough call to get an approval from an Aussie bloke, us Aussie men aren't really known for expressing ourselves. I really hope that the letter and my behaviour today makes her see me as a better option than Laurence and that shitting awful haircut of his. I have probably said more than I should've in the letter but I am desperate for her.

I press the call button on my phone for the fifth time in a row. Where the hell is Chad? I've rung him and sent him numerous texts. I can't wait to tell him what happened, he'll piss himself laughing. I promised him a few beers today as well to help us both get settled in the U.K. and enjoy the pub scene here, well until 8pm anyway as we have that absurd curfew to abide by. I still haven't worked up the guts to ask Uncle Terry why he has set such a ridiculous rule. The no girls, I can understand but it would be nice for a young bloke like me to experience some of the nightlife on the weekend and come back before 2am. I'm nearly thirty now and with looks to rival Cinderella's, I like to make it home before midnight before I look in the mirror and see a beer bloated pumpkin and feel like shit the next day.

I tried to ask Mum about it all when I last called her but all she said was that Uncle Terry just has a 'few weird ways about him' and I shouldn't worry about it. She wouldn't elaborate further, meaning she knows something I don't and wants me to work it out myself, (my mother has a habit of doing things like this – for example rather than telling me she had a new boyfriend, like any normal person she let me discover a whole load of men's clothes scattered along the house leading to her bedroom door. Luckily I worked out what this meant before I actually opened her door.) Or I suppose she might have been distracted by that muppet of a boyfriend of hers who can't even open a can of beans without having a full-on meltdown. Apparently, it is one of the things you must put up with when you are dating a 'young actor'. I'd tell her to seek help but it's a bit difficult to suggest that when she already is a psychologist specialising in romantic relationships, and knowing my own track record, who am I to judge.

After I practically skipped the whole way from Epping to Bethnal Green, leaving Chad a few more bumbling voicemails on his phone I arrive back at the flat. As soon as I enter I shout out Chad's name as if I am looking for a lost puppy. No response. Where the hell has he gone? It is then I notice a scrawled note on the back of a supermarket receipt. I instantly know it is Chad's handwriting as this guy makes a Doctor's scribbles look neat. It takes me a moment to decipher what he has written but it seems to say something along the lines of:

'Hey dude. Bored waiting for you, gone out on my own to see if I can catch myself a Pommie. See ya later.'

I instantly feel bad for leaving Chad on his own for most of the day, okay Chad is a full grown adult but it would've be nice to hang out together and chill with a couple of beers this evening.

'Hiccup'.

The sound makes me jump out of my skin.

'Hiccup'.

What the... I quickly check behind me to make sure I did close the front door and I haven't allowed one of the local tramps to walk in. Nope, the door is firmly closed. As I turn around to see where this noise could be coming from, I am confronted by a slightly overweight man with receding black hair slicked back from his face and a whole load of chest hair sprouting out of a silk dressing robe. Bloody hell. It's Uncle Terry, it looks like he might have gone on a bit of a bender last night, he looks horrendous.

'Ah, Ralph you're back...' he says while clutching his head, trying to remember my name, although incorrectly.

'Umm Uncle Terry, it's Ryan. In fact, you've been calling me Ryan since I got here, so not sure what's up with the name change.'

'Just a slip of the tongue boy, we all make mistakes don't we… Christ my head is killing me right now,' he says as he puts his head in his hands.

'Are you not feeling well Uncle Terry?'

The symptoms are adding up to a skinful last night, and considering he didn't invite us out with him because of his bloody curfew, I'm going to have some fun with him. Maybe not too much fun though as I do really need a place to stay, especially as my chances might be up with Ruby.

'Just a little Ryan, I think it might have been something I ate…'

Yeah right and my mother's the Queen of Sheba.

'Or maybe it was something you drunk Uncle Terry?'

'Hmmm, quite possibly, I am sure a paracetamol will fix things though… errr what on earth is this?'

Uncle Terry points to a post-it note that is stuck to the cabinet above the kitchen sink. The note has a stick drawing of what appears to be a woman with a crown and dress on, with a caption underneath that says 'Terry you are the best queen ever…'

'Is this some sort of joke Ralph… err I mean Ryan.'

The handwriting is certainly not mine and I know it's not Chad's either, in fact it looks a little bit like Uncle Terry's but I am certainly not going to suggest that to him.

'I swear on my mother and your sister's life that this is nothing to do with me, and neither is it Chad. In fact, here's some evidence of his handwriting here,' I say pointing to the scrawled receipt in my hand.

He takes a closer look at the receipt and then eyes me up and down before inspecting the post it note in his hands and I swear that I see his eyes widen almost in shock.

'Hmmm... okay well never mind about that now. Let's move on from this and get on with the rest of the day.'

I wasn't the one who started it. My Sherlock detective skills really are pointing towards him being the culprit, but I decide to keep schtum especially as I am beginning to feel guilty about the flowers I took earlier, let's hope he doesn't notice. Uncle Terry screws up the note and places it in the pocket of his silk night gown. He opens the cupboard where he scrabbles around inside throwing boxes of plasters and sachets of Lemsip into the sink in the process.

'Come on there must be some sort of painkiller in here.' He scrabbles around some more causing a whole bottle of cough syrup to fall and smash into several pieces in the sink below.

'Oh bloody hell.'

Watching a severely hungover man trying to do the simplest task is hilarious. The look on his face trying so desperately hard to locate something is priceless. Oh shit, I think I may be in trouble again...

'Ryan, seeing as you are standing here not being of much help, make yourself useful and get your poor Uncle some paracetamol from the supermarket down the road. In fact, while you are there, you might as well get my shopping for the next couple of days too. I'm hoping that my appetite will return later and I can cook us all my signature Teriyaki chicken again.

I must admit Uncle Terry's Teriyaki chicken is simply THE best and it makes this unnecessary trip to the supermarket a bit more bearable, even though we did eat it yesterday and I have just had a massive meal for lunch. It also sounds like the best thing to get Uncle Terry back to normal after his bout of illness 'fakeitis', more commonly known as 'hangover'.

Uncle Terry tears out a page from his notepad and hands it to me and as I look at the list of items, it confirms what I already thought; that Uncle Terry did write that other note. His drinking must have been of epic proportions last night. My stomach begins to rumble despite the fact I had a humungous roast chicken lunch, so I head back out of the door and away from Uncle Terry's continuous groaning.

And just before the door closes Uncle Terry croaks out;

'Where have my lilies gone?'

I quickly slam the door shut and make a mental note to get some replacement flowers, clearly he wasn't as hungover as I thought.

***

In the supermarket I quickly find most of the items Uncle Terry needs, all I am looking for now is some rice and flowers and then I am out of here, quicker than Usain Bolt at the Olympics and ready to stuff my face with a whole load more food, this boy can never say no to more food.

I hate supermarkets at the best of times, they are always full of dawdlers, you know those people who stand daydreaming in the middle of the aisle for about ten minutes, normally right where you need to get your items, thinking about how they wish to make a pumpkin, cranberry and red onion tagine, but instead they head straight to the takeaway aisle and get the Indian special for ten pounds. Then there are the mothers with screaming toddlers, y'know the ones who decide their child sounds like an air raid siren, so the mother decides to vacate the area leaving everyone else to deal with the noise as they skip around the aisles as if they are still a single and fresh faced twenty-year-old despite the sick stain down their top. If there is such a thing as hell on earth then I think the supermarket is the place.

I scan the dried goods aisle more efficiently than Blade Runner and pick up the coveted packet of rice and just as I turn around to make my escape out of the labyrinth and to the till, I smash right into a woman who also was trying to get to the rice. I apologise immediately, feeling slightly embarrassed that I didn't see her whilst trying to be a stealthy rice grabbing ninja. Not going to lie, this girl is pretty attractive with brown shoulder length hair, big blue eyes and an ass that is riper than a juicy peach.

'Really sorry doll. I didn't mean to bump into you like that.'

'Oh no, it's all my fault I was in my own little daydream as usual. I am ever so sorry about that… Anyways no harm done. I guess like me, you are shopping for one?' she says as she gives a little pout and twiddles her silky brown hair in her left-hand to suggest we could have dinner for two and maybe even dessert if I play my cards right.

I think about how easy it would be to have a bit of fun with this girl, just to keep the motor tickin', just to show that I've still got it. Then my brain flashes back to Tanya, I remember the trouble these types of flings had got me in the past and I don't want to have another girl causing issues in my life, moving to London is a fresh new start and the chance of love not lust.

'Nah, this stuff is for me and my Uncle Terry.'

She immediately looks horrified and quickly scuttles off. I then realise how much of a creep I sound by saying I'm just buying dinner for my Uncle and I. It's lucky I am not wearing a mac and have bad personal hygiene, just to really finish off the creep look. I shrug my shoulders at the lost opportunity and continue to make my way to the till grabbing a bunch of half-decent looking flowers on the way and as I do so I spot the same girl again and I see her eyes widen as I put the flowers in my basket. By this point I don't care whether she thinks I am on a date with a guy called Terry or that I lied to her and actually meeting another girl. I know I only have one woman who is deserving of my wandering hands all over her body, and as something has just gone ping in my trouser pocket, which isn't anatomy based, I think I may have received a message from that said woman.

CHAPTER 9

How do I respond to that. That letter full of love and hope. It's heart-breaking but also heart-warming. I never thought anyone would say anything like that to me ever. In fact I can't even imagine Laurence being this brutally honest to me about how he feels.

What can I write back to a man who has poured his whole entire heart out on the page to me and told me he loves me? I was an idiot for running off like that and not allowing him to explain himself, but after everything that happened to me in Sydney, my head wasn't in a good place. I needed time to process things and maybe in a weird way it was the Universe's way of telling me that I wasn't destined to be with Ryan, it is Laurence that I need to be with.

I had waited so long for someone to love me, someone who would care for me, someone who wanted to be with me forever. I waited for years to experience love and then just like my mother's favourite hackneyed saying 'You wait all day for a bus and then two come along at the same time.' And as much as I hate that phrase, it seems to neatly sum up my love life. However, now that I am on one bus it looks like the other bus is still chasing me down the road.

I can't just tell Ryan to 'fuck off' and never get in contact again so that I can carry on as normal and enjoy my life here with Laurence and building up my floristry business. I am sure if Martha was here, she would've told him that the opportunity had gone, yet she was the one who gave him my address, I guess she didn't think that my relationship with Laurence would end up being so serious. Oh how I ache for Martha, she knows me better than anyone and when she isn't here it's like there is something missing, a bond that no lover or best friend can ever understand or ever replicate. I wonder if she can feel my anguish now and I wonder if she ever has doubts about her life with Chloe in Australia.

There has always been this unwritten rule between us. We talk to each other about every emotion that we experience, except one - Love. I think we would hurt each other too much to know that one of us was pining deeply for the feel and touch of love of another. That is probably why I was so distant from Martha during our time in Sydney, one of us had found love and the other was still searching and maybe still is. We know our love as twins is strong, and to try and search for another mate to complete our happiness in the world is a treacherous path that we need to tread alone.

I suppose that is one positive to take out of the mess I appeared to have found myself in, no matter what is loved and lost between Ryan and even Laurence, the connection and love I have for my sister can never be torn apart. We are one. Oh Martha, I really hope we are reunited again soon.

I stare back at the now crumpled letter in my hand. Everything was going so well before he arrived, everything seemed so much straightforward and wonderful but there is still this dull ache for something more. Ryan and I can't be together but at the same time I don't want him out of my life. There is a connection there and I don't want to lose it so I will keep things short and sweet in a text to him, showing I care but only as a friend.

Okay let's try this as a response:

```
Those words were beautiful. I miss you. Yours
Ruby. X
```

Woah, that is way too much, my typing fingers are betraying me and writing things that could lead to all sorts of emotional trouble. Where did that thought even come from? I am going to blame my hormones for thinking that was a good idea to send to someone who is just a friend. I quickly delete the message from my phone. That was a close one. I still can't believe I typed that. Okay, let's try again.

```
Nice to see you. Thanks for letter. R.
```

Okay now I just sound like a cold-hearted bitch. How can writing a message to a friend be so bloody hard! Right, third time lucky…

```
Hey Ryan, it was so lovely to see you earlier and
that letter you sent was very touching. Hopefully
see you at the opening night of the Lemon Tree.
Your friend Ruby. Xx
```

That sounds much better, ensuring we stay in contact by offering to meet up at my opening night but also making it very clear we are to just be friends. It's not stringing him along or is it? It's too late now, my impulses have caused me to press send before I have time to think about it anymore. I think I've said the right things and made it clear that I can only reciprocate his love with friendship. Yet for some reason deep down I feel like my heart wants to go on another rollercoaster ride. I won't let it. This thought needs to be buried, along with the relationship that was never meant to be.

CHAPTER 10

'Your friend Ruby'. Every time I read that message, these words sting harder. I once said them to her and knew how much they would hurt, and now here she is uttering them back to me. Well at least she is talking to me I suppose. I should have been more realistic, a piece of paper can't make someone fall in love with you on the spot although I wish it did.

I eventually reply back to her message. No more games, no more pretending to be bachelor of the year, I am just going to be me. The soppy, idiot of a man who sometimes is good at using spreadsheets for his job and just wants to be loved. And surprisingly I am happy with that, even if my description of myself is something you would use to re-home a dog with.

Ping. She's messaged back straight away and I immediately look at what she has written and think how best to reply before eagerly responding. They need to change my name to Dan. Desperate Dan.

The text conversation between us is light but she does reply every time I ping her over a message. I never respond to friends that quickly or maybe I am just clutching at straws thinking she could be interested. She seems pretty happy with this new fella even though he looks a bit like an 80s Jason Donavan. Despite looking like a prick, she's stayed loyal to him and in a way that makes me love her even more, and makes me realise what a fucking tool I really was when I was dating her.

I lay on my bed, wallowing in my own misery, thinking about all the idiotic things I've done in the last couple of years and how I should really apologise to all those girls I treated like shit just to satisfy my own needs. Chad, my Mum, even my slightly estranged father used to tell me to get my act together when it came to women, and how I wished I listened to them before it was too late. The call of lust was just too strong. I let out a sigh and tell myself the misery phase needs to be over. It's time to get positive and move on. I pull my phone out of my jean pocket to find out what time it is and realise it is now midnight. What I thought was just an hour of misery was in fact six hours of self-loathing, and I begin to hate myself even more for letting myself continue this one person pity party for so long.

It's a Sunday night and even though I don't start work until next week, it is definitely time for me to get some sleep and finally get over this horrific jet lag. I don't know why my body is taking so long to adjust, I am even considering people's suggestions online to place teaspoons on the back of my knees to see if this sorts out my body clock. I rub my tired yet still wide awake eyes and begin to take my jeans and t-shirt off ready for bed but as I do so I can hear a scratching noise that sounds like it is coming from the front door, followed by a clicking noise and the sound of someone falling over followed by whispers.

I'm pretty sure Uncle Terry is in bed, especially as he was the one who imposed that stupid curfew on us over the weekend, even on a Sunday evening, I mean who goes out on a fucking Sunday night for Christ sake. Although Chad has clearly gone somewhere tonight as he wasn't here for Teriyaki chicken, I am sure he would've come in before curfew time, there were still a few minutes before it was officially curfew time before I headed to my room so I'm sure Chad would've made it back just in time. He might look like a surf bum but he is pretty good at following

80

the rules when he needs to. Despite appearances he was actually in the junior cadets at school and won an award for being the 'most disciplined cadet.' That only leaves me with one option, we are being burgled. Fuck.

I look around my bedroom to see if there is anything I can use to arm myself against these intruders. I've heard stories from other Aussies and Kiwis in London that the crime rate is pretty high with stabbings and shootings happening on a daily basis in London, but I just shrugged them off as rumours, thinking that the place is probably no different to Sydney but clearly I was wrong. Fuck fuckety fuck. The only things I can find in my room to protect myself is my pillow and some trainers. I'm sure they are a great defence against a bunch of Care Bears but fucking useless against a knife-wielding attacker. There's never a baseball bat in sight when you need them, probably because Hollywood keeps buying them up.

I am just going to have to hope that those press ups I've been doing each morning will mean I am slightly stronger than these intruders and can overpower them before they do any damage. I did sixty two and a half press ups the other day and my arms are still killing me.

I slowly open my bedroom door just enough so there is a small crack I can see through to suss out the area. I feel like Tom Cruise in *Mission: Impossible*, although I'm pretty sure he never had to complete any missions in just his jocks. I feel my breathing getting shallower and my heartbeat getting louder in my chest. My eyes take a while to adjust to the darkness of the living room but I can begin to make out two shadows and as suspected, one appears to be male, the other female. It looks like the male is wearing shorts, who an earth would wear shorts in this bloody weather, it's almost on the verge of snowing here. Then it dawns on me. Chad. Chad would be the only one crazy enough to go out and wear shorts no matter what the weather, he is also much bloody stupider than I thought, I blame that stupid bitch ex-girlfriend for messing him up like this.

I go back and turn off my bedroom light and pick up my phone to use the torch on it, to doubly confirm that it is Chad as I don't want to jump too quickly to conclusions and end up suffocated by my own pillow. I place the light in the crack of the door and see it is definitely Chad. Thank God. However, it appears that he has now lost his shorts and is just in his jocks, his female companion has also lost a considerable amount of clothing too and is now spread-eagled over my Uncle's dining table, almost knocking off the replacement flowers I bought Uncle Terry. Jeez did I get a bollocking for that, serves me right I suppose as I should have asked although I was going to replace them… eventually. I watch as the vase gets closer and closer to the edge and I can't take it anymore.

This needs to come to an end right now. I bloody hope Uncle Terry got drunk again and is now comatose in bed recovering, or at the very least is extremely hard of hearing during the night time and hasn't heard any of this, otherwise the pair of us are going to be finding ourselves homeless pretty quickly. How could Chad do this? Uncle Terry is basically putting us up for free in London the most expensive capital in the world and all we have to do was follow two fucking stupid rules.

I open the door wider and shine the phone torchlight right in their direction, yet they carry on having a good time, ignoring the fact it has suddenly got lighter in the room.

'Chad,' I whisper loudly. He still hasn't twigged I can see exactly what he is up to, so I decide to creep a little closer and hope he doesn't yelp out in surprise.

'Psst Chad. What the fuck are you doing?'

'Oh hey Ryan! Just showing my friend here a good time.' Chad is completely and utterly wasted and his female companion looks a little worse for wear as well. She looks at me in just my pants, whilst she is still spread-eagled on the table and gives me a wink. I feel my face go red with embarrassment. God knows where Chad found this woman but whatever hole she crawled out of, she needs to crawl back into it as she cannot be here. However before I do anything else I move the flowers to the nearby coffee table out of harm's way and that helps bring my blood pressure down just a tiny bit, I then go back to the situation at hand.

'Chad, you know that you can't bring girls back here, remember what Terry told us?'

'Ah yeah TEZZA. Good ol' TEZZA. SUCH A TOP BLOKE.'

I suddenly resume the motions of an air traffic controller and wave my arms up and down in the hope it makes Chad pipe the fuck down. Uncle Terry better have industrial strength ear plugs in.

'Look Chad, I am sure you and this… er…' I look back at this woman still grinning at me. She is an absolute mess, and I am struggling to find a word to describe her without being offensive…

'…yes you and your lady friend here are having a great time but here is really not the time or place, so how about you get this er… lady friend of yours a taxi and you can catch up tomorrow over coffee or something.'

'Piss off Ryan, just 'cause you're jealous that I've got a Pommie to shag tonight and you don't.'

Ooh that was a low blow, even for a drunk Chad. To be fair I am beginning to sound 'holier than thou' by telling him to stop being such an arse tonight, whereas I know that the old me would not have given a shit about anyone else just to get laid but times have changed, dare I say it I may actually be acting like a grown up rather than a tosser who needs to stick his dick into any woman in sight.

'Look Chad, I don't care who you sleep with as long as it is not here as quite frankly I need a roof over my head. Now get her out of here pronto.'

This is the first time I have ever had to get angry at Chad, but this is the first time he has truly crossed the line.

'Boys. Is that you?'.

Oh shitting hell. Looks like I am going to be on the news tomorrow as the Boxer Short Man of Bethnal Green, with footage of me scrambling around in my undies trying to find a suitable cardboard box to sleep in.

The sound of Terry's voice sobers Chad up immediately, he's gone from a warm pink colour to an ashen grey. I need to act fast if we have any chance of still living here by the morning.

I quickly grab the girl off the table by the arm, who, despite the commotion, is still just in her bra and skirt, and drag her to the front door. As expected she is not willing to go that easily, she is pulling away from my grip and is scratching her cheap acrylic nails across my skin, on the verge of drawing blood, but at this moment in time my adrenaline is too high to feel the pain. My mind is on overdrive trying to think of an excuse we can tell Uncle Terry that will land us in lukewarm water rather than steaming hot water and homeless.

I have a lightbulb moment.

'WALTZING MATILDA... WALTZING MATILDA... YOU'LL COME A WALTZING MATILDA WITH ME...'

Chad is initially perplexed, but through his drunken haze he still appears to have faith in me and decides to join in with the singing. I am really hoping that Matilda will save our bacon when it comes to being roasted by Uncle Terry.

In what feels like an eternity but is probably just a few seconds, the woman stops scratching my arms, probably because she is starting to lose some of her acrylic nails, and I seize my opportunity to push her out the front door of the apartment and, just as I do, Uncle Terry appears in the room. He looks rather angrily at us both, although I am finding it hard to keep a straight face as he is wearing a hairnet, a pair of pink fluffy slippers and a silk dressing robe. He looks absolutely ridiculous. If it wasn't for the fact that my entire life feels like it is on the line I would be rolling on the floor with laughter, I just hope Chad manages to remain composed as well.

I continue singing at the top of my voice and so does Chad, we are not out of the clear yet as that bloody woman is now shouting and banging on the front door.

Shit. Now I know why. Her t-shirt. As if I haven't been punished enough this evening, I see that the small scrap of material is literally inches away from one of Uncle Terry's fluffy slippers. I nudge Chad and give him the eye and subtly point my head at the piece of cloth on the floor. He gives me a nod back to confirm he understands there is an issue and he has to deal with it, our rendition of Waltzing Matilda is still going strong and as it does, Uncle Terry's folded arms are getting tighter and tighter and I worry he might explode any minute.

Chad however, moves towards this ticking time-bomb as if he wants to waltz with him across the floor which unfortunately results in the explosion of Detonator Terry 3000…

'WHAT AN EARTH ARE YOU DOING BOYS?' Uncle Terry bellows back to us, whilst at the same time pushing Chad out of the way and bulldozing straight to my direction.

As he does so I see that Chad dives over the t-shirt as if he is practising for the Rugby World Cup. Maybe I shouldn't have let a drunk bloke deal with this issue…

Uncle Terry is walking closer to me and I slowly move sideways across the wall to get some distance from the door, to give Chad the opportunity to get rid of the offending item and to make Uncle Terry less aware of the danger zone.

'WE ARE JUST INDULGING IN SOME AUSTRALIAN CULTURE… Y'KNOW TO REMIND US OF HOME AND LET PEOPLE KNOW HOW GREAT STRAYA IS.'

I hear the door open but I refuse to look in that direction in case it encourages Uncle Terry to do the same and he decides to throw us out there with that screaming banshee.

'CAN YOU PLEASE NOT SHOUT RYAN. IT IS TOTALLY UNNECESSARY.'

I take a moment to see if I can hear anything and whether I need to pretend I am hard of hearing. Silence. Thank God the screaming banshee has finally finished battering down the door. Chad comes to stand next to me and gives me the nod that all is well. It's funny how a simple nod between men can explain so much.

'Sorry Uncle Terry. Just feeling a bit emotional tonight, just missing the motherland I 'spose.'

'Look, I know you boys are a long way from home but you need to be an adult about it. You're twenty-nine for god's sake Ryan. You've also broken the curfew of being out of your room before 2am, you are very lucky I wasn't…'

He suddenly pauses and I take the opportunity to jump in with a grovelling apology;

'You're right Uncle Terry, sorry about all that. I don't really know what came over me. I promise that won't happen again.'

I glare at Chad, if it wasn't for him I wouldn't be snivelling up to Uncle Terry like some naughty school boy being caught by the head teacher smoking behind the bike sheds.

'I have a pack of Tim Tams in the cupboard that your Mum gave me a while back. How about we open them tomorrow and have them with a cup of coffee and you can tell me what you boys have been up to this weekend. Does that sound like a good idea?'

'Thanks Uncle Terry, that sounds grand.'

'Cheers Tez… erm… Terry. I love a good Tim Tam.'

Then just as he is about to turn back to his bedroom allowing me to breathe a sigh of relief, he then seems to realise something and swivels fully back in my direction, looks me up and down and says;

'What in God's name happened to your arm?'

'Ah it's nothing really, I think I just got bitten by a gnat or something and I'm unfortunately a bit of a scratcher, clearly these Pommie gnats love a bit of Aussie blood.'

I try to put on a brave face, despite the fact that now the adrenaline has worn off I feel like half my arm has been chopped off.

'Hmmm well make sure you close all the windows and doors in future if you see those horrible things again, I don't want some dirty bug drinking my precious blood… right I think it is time for bed for all of us. Goodnight boys.'

'Goodnight Uncle Terry,' we chime in unison.

He tightens the belt on his dressing gown, gives his hairnet a quick pat and pirouettes back in the direction of his bedroom. Chad and I then await for the large thwacking sound made by his slippers to stop before we make another sound.

I'm pretty sure something isn't quite right with Uncle Terry, I swear just the other day he was playing the greatest hits of Judy Garland in his room, but whatever. I'm glad he is still keeping a roof over our heads, for tonight at least. I just need to get Chad in to line to ensure this doesn't happen again.

'I've been a fucking idiot, haven't I Ryan.'

'Just a little bit mate yeah. Maybe next time go back to the girls place rather than coming here, or maybe just bring back the old Chad and not the one that thinks he is on *The Bachelor*. From personal experience I know these one night stands do not lead to good things.'

'Yeah sorry dude. I don't know what's the matter with me recently. I think losing Charlie has hit me hard. I just need some time I think to sort my head out. Like I said I'm sorry... and thanks for saving us tonight.'

'Don't worry Chad, that's what friends are for. Let's grab lunch out together tomorrow and we can just have a chat about things and maybe work out why Uncle Terry is so fond of a hairnet.'

Chad lets out a small smile and makes his way towards his room but before he does so he turns and says;

'Thanks Ryan, you're a great mate. I hope you know that.'

'Thanks mate. See ya tomorrow.'

'Night buddy.'

I enter my room ready to finally get some rest, but before my head hits the pillow I am already dreaming of being back in Sydney with the Chad I used to know and the girl I used to have.

CHAPTER 11

So this is it. I push the key into the door and after jangling it around a few times, I manage to get the door open and I enter into the empty space. My shop. My future. I take a moment to stand in the middle and admire all the space I have to create my vision for The Lemon Tree. The shop feels bigger than the last time I was here and I begin to panic whether I will have enough stock and displays to fill the vast space. Laurence must have sensed my anxiety as he comes up behind me and places his warm hands on my shoulders and gives them a quick squeeze.

'Babe, you're going to make this shop look cracking.'

He then plants a soft kiss at the base of my neck before heading back outside in order to unload the van, full of the shop equipment and also our own personal stuff. Despite being packed in separate boxes, after all the shaking around in the van and the fact that Laurence thinks he is Michael Schumacher, it wouldn't surprise me if my pyjamas are in my plant pots and my bulbs are in my wash bag.

Thankfully there are no actual flowers or other fresh stock in the van as these are arriving in a few days, meaning I will have just a few hours before the shop opens for its first day of trading to add the flowers and make it perfect. It will be hard work, but as my dad likes to remind me, the only time success comes before work is in the dictionary. Dad loves giving out such gems of advice, although I don't think he expects to receive numerous eye rolls in response or Martha's favourite saying; 'Thanks Captain Obvious.' I know he means well though.

The move is even more of a big deal as Laurence and I are officially moving in together in the flat above the shop. We thought it would be for the best as our relationship is ready to move to the next level, and it means I can be available at any time to deal with the business. I've spent nights at Laurence's flat so it won't be a complete shock when he starts parading around the flat in his SpongeBob SquarePants boxers, but there is always that worry at the back of my mind that maybe it won't work out.

I hear the lift of shutters behind me and I see that Laurence has already sprung into action opening the back of the van, I quickly go out to help but as I do so, he suddenly climbs into the van, ignoring the boxes right in front of him and dives towards the very far end. He then mumbles;

'Goddammit. I should've kept it with me instead of packing it away. It's going to take me ages to find my tech box… ah hang on.'

Please don't tell me he is actually trying to get his laptop out, that is the last of our worries right now.

After some rather rough handling, he suddenly jumps up and shouts out;

'Bazinga!! And the charger is there as well. Today is going to be a good day.'

He better have a bloody good reason as to why he needs his laptop, otherwise he will find that charging cable of his will do more than just charge.

As he climbs back out of the van and dusts himself down, looking mightily pleased with himself, I ask him why he needs his laptop right now.

'I've got something important I need to do,' he says as he hustles quickly past me and inside the shop.

He has something important he needs to do. He has got to be fucking kidding me. What is more important right now that he needs to do on that wretched machine of his than helping me set up shop? He said he would help, in fact he promised. I try to calm myself down and tell myself maybe it's my hormones and the stress of starting my own business that are making his behaviour seem ridiculous and that I just need to get over it. I promised myself I would never be one of those whingeing girlfriends, and so far in the relationship I think I am doing a pretty good job, although he is really testing the limit right now.

Laurence suddenly turns back around, and I wonder whether he has suddenly realised that he is treading in deep water right now with a girl who might turn into Medusa at any moment.

'Also Rubes, would you mind fetching me a fold-up chair to sit on whilst I am on my laptop.'

Sure you can have a chair, once I've slammed it across your back like those wrestlers on the TV. I am genuinely wondering if he is just taking the piss right now but his face tells me otherwise. I stare at him for what seems to be eternity just to check he is being for real and in the hope he might realise that this behaviour really isn't acceptable.

'You do know where the chair is in the van don't you?'

I don't even offer a response and walk away, my hands gripped so tightly I am beginning to leave nail marks in my palms. I find his rotten goddamn chair and take it out of the van and throw it towards his general direction for him to deal with.

'Hey… there's no need to be like that…'

I give him the silent treatment and again walk away back to the van and begin collecting the rest of the stuff. I hate being so angry at him but he has really crossed the line, I needed his help today and he seems to think playing computer games are a higher priority. I can't even look or speak to him right now and it is best I don't as I might end up saying something I later regret.

Luckily Andre and Catrina are coming along later so hopefully they can boost my spirits and give me a hand. In a sadistic way, I am hoping that Catrina is in a feisty mood and will give Laurence an earful for being such a lazy boyfriend right now.

The first box I lift from the van feels like I am carrying a dead weight but I am determined to carry it and I deliberately walk slowly huffing and puffing right past where Laurence is sitting in order to make a point that he should be assisting.

'Can you not come so close Ruby, you are blocking the light on my screen.'

I drop the box immediately, shocked at the audacity of this man and in return it lands right on my foot, causing me to howl in pain and let out the devil woman.

'DON'T YOU THINK YOU SHOULD BE HELPING ME INSTEAD OF PLAYING YOUR SHITTY COMPUTER GAME OF DUNGEONS AND DEMONS. YOU'RE ACTING LIKE A TWELVE YEAR OLD RATHER THAN BEING A FULLY GROWN MAN.'

Laurence looks like a rabbit caught in the headlights, frightened to see that his once respectable girlfriend has turned into this evil harridan woman who might burst into flames at any moment.

'I think you are referring to the game Dungeons and Dragons, there is no such thing as Dungeons and Demons, besides that is an offline game. World of Warcraft is the game I play online.'

I let out a scream of frustration right in Laurence's face, which causes him to stand up from his chair and place his hands on my wrists in order to contain me and keep me calm, plus I think he was a little concerned I might just fly at him and destroy his beloved laptop. In fact I am starting to wonder whether he loves that laptop more than he does me.

'Calm down Ruby.'

He looks at me cool and controlled and despite what has happened between us, his bright blue eyes and his warm hands on my wrists make me catch my breath. In that moment I feel my eyes begin to water and then my shoulders begin to move up and down as I sob uncontrollably.

Laurence quickly releases my wrists and pulls me in closer and wraps one arm round my waist as his other hand begins to gently rub my back.

'Shhh, it's okay Ruby, this whole moving thing and starting your own business can be stressful. I realise me being on my laptop looks like a real shitty thing to be doing but I was so desperate to get this thing finished before we got cracking with setting up the shop... and in fact with just a few tweaks it will be. Actually... you know what I might as well show you now...'

He takes me over to his laptop and as I wipe away the tears from my eyes, I see the words 'The Lemon Tree' emblazoned across the screen, causing me to blink a few times to check that what I am seeing is real. It looks like a website, and not just any website, one of those really professional ones, something that looks

94

straight out of a lifestyle magazine, it is truly stunning.

'So I thought I would get The Lemon Tree set up on the virtual world with a website. I hope you don't mind.'

'Oh wow, Laurence this looks incredible. I don't mind at all. It makes The Lemon Tree look much more amazing than it does in reality.'

'Well that's not all.'

He does a few clicks with his mouse and up comes a whole array of social media sites set up just for the shop, all of which look so aesthetically pleasing and pretty, although it is making me feel more anxious than I already am, as I'm worried the shop won't live up to the hype. Somehow I already have hundreds of followers already, I can hardly breathe. This shop, this adventure it is all becoming too real.

'I thought a shop that is destined to be successful in the real world, should also have a chance in the virtual world.'

Laurence says this to me with his puppy-eyes in full pleading and 'please like me' mode and I suddenly feel tremendously guilty for my behaviour earlier. I shouldn't have jumped to conclusions like that. Jumping to conclusions has got me into trouble before. I should have trusted that Laurence was helping me in some way but sometimes his behaviour can be so irrational, it leaves me really frustrated and sometimes very lonely in that I can't fathom out what he is thinking or how he is really feeling. I try to express my gratitude of how I feel about this brilliant set up to him by giving him a long embrace that he willingly accepts and nuzzles my neck in return. Although despite my attempt at a warm embrace, deep down I am so scared that this is going to go wrong, not just the shop but us too, I want to tell him this but I just can't find the words and find it easier to put on a brave face.

'I'm sorry that I got so mad with you, this is just brilliant. Thank you so much.'

'And I am sorry for being a dick and not telling you what I was up to, I just wanted it to be a surprise,' he says as he lets go of our embrace and looks directly into my eyes.

'And I'm Andre but you guys already knew that.'

Andre pops his bearded head in between Laurence and I and lets out a cheesy grin, which after the initial shock makes us all laugh.

'Quit clowning around you lot, we've got work to do' bellows Catrina, the voice of reason.

'But that doesn't mean that work can't be fun.'

Andre pulls out a feather duster from the heavy box I brought in, and begins to sashay around the shop swinging his hips and pouting his lips.

Catrina rolls her eyes and we are all smiles and all ready to begin making plans as to how best to bring in the boxes, and get the shop and flat set up as soon as possible. The moment of madness that I just experienced already becomes a distant memory as we all begin to chip in to make this the best shop ever.

I think Laurence is right, today will be a good day. No more distractions and misunderstandings. It's just flowers, friends and my beautiful boyfriend.

CHAPTER 12

I'm still waiting for that text. That text that tells me for definite that she still wants me and has lost interest in Laurence. Instead the only information I have had from her over the past week are invites to join her online newsletter, Facebook Page, Instagram and Twitter for 'The Lemon Tree', and to be honest if I carry on liking, retweeting and sharing her stuff I am going to look like a right lemon as well. All I want is for her to slide into my DM's and say; 'Hey, thanks Ryan for the likes. I like you too!' So much for the old Ryan not giving a shit about anyone's feelings or opinions. Now I finally understand why girls get pissed off when they don't get a text. Karma really is a bitch.

Although my personal life has always been a mess, my work life has always been on tip top form. I was continually the best performing accountant at Charter and Charter in Sydney and it is something that I hope to continue whilst in London. It just happened they were looking for someone in the Sydney office to assist in the office in London, so I thought I might as well seize the opportunity as it also gives me more time to win back Ruby and get her to come back to Australia with me. Besides the last person who came to London was given partnership when they returned so I am hoping the same will happen to me, the only problem is that I can't seem to find the bloody building where I'm working. I probably should have spent my last week finding this place instead of being Chad's counsellor. I always thought Chad was an easy going guy, I had no idea how cut up he really was about breaking up with Charlie and I also had no idea that when he cries and blows his nose it sounds as if I stepped into the middle of an elephant enclosure.

Thankfully I left the flat in plenty of time today in order to find the office. In my head I thought I would easily find the building, grab myself a turmeric latte in a café opposite, before suavely making my way into the office with my suit jacket slung over my back ready to do business and show everyone how awesome I am. Okay I probably wouldn't act like such a dick, but it would be nice to get some coffee to keep me alert and warm in these arctic conditions.

All the buildings and streets in Canary Wharf look the same, all full of skyscrapers and men and women walking briskly in navy suits. I try not to get too distracted by the city landscape as I need to find King Edward Street pronto otherwise I could be fired before I even begin my work here. Clients and professionalism come first, lateness is not acceptable. I really should have come down last week to suss the place out, instead of wasting time thinking of Ruby, sorting out Chad and watching episodes of a programme called *Countdown*, although I always managed to get the math questions right in the time, just a shame this doesn't help me now.

I have gone into three buildings so far, all of them towering glass monstrosities; all of their foyers consists of one random piece of modern art, all had white walls, probably because they spent so much money on the art and couldn't afford any other paint than white, and all of them have an idiotic woman named Karen on reception. Asking them for directions to Charter and Charter is like asking a dead fish to show you how to get to the ocean. Absolutely bloody useless and are nothing more than an ornament to stop the place looking so empty.

After being given directions that roughly consisted of being asked to turn around, stand on my head and sing 'Agadoo', I take a deep breath and try not to have a panic attack. I reach for my phone and at this point realise I have been a fucking idiot. The answer was in my pocket all along. *Google Maps*. It's because I need a coffee, not the fact I am really nervous. Ryan Crichton is never nervous.

I type the address into my phone and wait a few seconds. The direction it sends me in, is to the building I am currently standing opposite. Un-fucking believable.

With the clock ticking I have no time to waste so, I enter the building, all sweaty and tired, the complete opposite of the first impression I wanted to give, and come face to face with another receptionist who lo and behold when I look at her name badge is called Karen as well. Why are they all called fucking Karen? I also see that behind her is a plastic plaque with Charter and Charter on it, allowing me to breathe a sigh of relief that *Google Maps* was right and I have reached my destination. I tell Karen that it is my first day here and that I am due to report to Neil at 8.30 am. I look at my watch and see that I am here dead on 8.30 am, surprisingly maintaining my record of never being late. Maybe there is a God.

Karen then uses her painted red claws to press a few buttons on the phone and gets through to Neil, I presume.

'Hi Babe, the new guy is here.'

I thought the English were more formal than us Aussies, as even back home Betty the bohemian from Byron Bay who worked on reception would never call anyone 'babe' in the workplace.

'Just take a seat and he will be down in a minute.'

She's only said a few words to me but I can already suss Karen's type out immediately, she's blatantly in her mid-forties but tries to convince everyone else that wearing a short black mini-skirt, low-cut white blouse and a bucket-load of paint on her face means she is still in her twenties. She probably also refers to her job not as a receptionist but as an 'Administrative Support Clerk' to make it seem more important than it actually is. I also bet she is one of those women who is down the pub on a Friday night telling the whole world and his dog that she 'don't need no man' but if a man with enough money and no common sense comes along, I'm sure she will be happy to swap sitting on her fat arse in reception for sitting on her fat arse in a big mansion in the countryside.

I attempt to make myself comfortable on the black leather seat in the foyer and peruse the magazines on offer on the glass table in front of me. These leather seats are the worst as they are the low rectangular type which means unless you are five foot or under they have no back support whatsoever and are the most uncomfortable waiting chairs ever, I presume chosen deliberately so you don't loiter here too long and enjoy staring at the tin foil cow that's been castrated in the name of art.

As I try and decide whether to read the Charter and Charter Health and Safety manual or Fly Fishing Today, I hear the receptionist shout out my name.

'Ryan…' she coos. 'I just wondered what you thought of my new glasses, do you think they make me look smart?'

She pops on a pair of black rectangle shaped spectacles, deliberately slides them to the end of her nose and leans over her desk to show her ageing cleavage. I weigh up whether to pretend not to hear her and feign a real interest in this fly fishing magazine. I reluctantly decide to give her my attention, just because it is my first day here and you never know who could be helpful in a new office like this. I word my response to show politeness but not enough to show I am interested in her, as quite frankly I'd rather make love to a plastic bag than her.

'They look very smart Karen.'

She flashes a toothy grin, thinking I have given her more of a compliment than what I have actually said.

'Neil says I look like a sexy librarian in them… Oooh talk of the devil, here he is.'

Thank Christ for that. I turn around and stand up to greet Neil… Oh shit, it's that Neil, the one who earned the nickname back home as 'Knobhead Neil' for the obvious reason he is a dick. Once people got bored of his dickish antics, he somehow arranged to move over to London. I completely forget he was here, although to be honest with his track record I'm surprised he hasn't been fired yet.

'Well well well Ryan, it appears that you seem to be chatting up our receptionist already. Not the greatest of first impressions is it?'

'Errr no, I wasn't doing that at all, I just said her glasses looked smart, nothing else. I'm just here to work Neil, not to cause a scene.'

'Oh please, we all know about your reputation at work.'

This guy is doing everything he can to wind me up in the hope he will make me explode but this Jack will be staying firmly in his box. I am good at my job and I refuse to have people like Neil ruin my chances of being successful here.

'You mean the reputation I have for being an excellent work colleague Neil, I presume that is what you are referring to?'

Ryan 1, Neil 0.

'Sure mate, you keep telling yourself that. Just keep your hands off my receptionist.'

As we begin to walk to the lifts, he suddenly turns around and gives Karen a wink and shouts; 'See you later, you saucy minx'. The whole of the foyer, which has suddenly gone from being empty to full of people dressed in business attire, all turn around to look at Neil and I, even Karen has gone the colour of a baked salmon from the embarrassment.

'What did I tell you about flirting with the receptionist. You really are a naughty boy aren't you RYAN?' He deliberately shouts my name so everyone now thinks I am the office pervert.

Ryan 1, Neil 1.

I decide that the best thing to do is just ignore Neil's ridiculous comments in the hope that he gives up trying to humiliate me. Thankfully the office is only three floors up so it should only be a short lift ride. He is pushing fifty now, although his face looks like a teenage boy's, full of grease and pimples, it's the receding hair line that gives away the age, it doesn't help that it has been slicked back to an inch of its life. I swear his hair was blonde, but now it looks like a dirty brown colour. He is just a couple of inches shorter than me, meaning I could possibly take him in a fight, which is looking more and more possible at this stage. He is also sporting quite a substantial middle age spread and to top it off, his breath smells like he has brushed his teeth with an onion.

'Welcome to level three' announces the lift voice. Thank god for that, I don't know how much longer I could've coped in being in such close proximity to that man, that lift ride went on longer than I thought. As we enter the office, I feel a little at ease as it reminds me of the set up back home. Apart from back home I didn't have 'Knobhead Neil' to cause me misery whilst at work.

'Ryan follow me..' barks Neil, to ensure I am still on his leash.

We walk towards the back of the office, ensuring Neil has paraded me around everyone on the floor.

'This is your desk here', he points with his chubby finger, despite the fact we are right next to it.

'You won't be sitting next to me as I am at the important end of the office.'

I think what he really means is he sits at the end where you don't get caught playing computer games instead of working.

'You'll be sitting next to Raj and Daniel, they can show you the ropes. I've got far too much to do to show people like you what to do.'

This guy is actually unbelievable, he is the same level as I am. He really has made himself King of the office. I swear I can actually see Raj shaking in his seat due to Neil standing so close to him. I look at Daniel and he is refusing to make eye contact with anyone, pretending to click things with his mouse, despite the fact his screen isn't even turned on.

'Oh and by the way, some of us go out on Saturday evening for some drinks at the local just round the corner, although it can be a bit of a large one. It's pretty much compulsory so I expect to see you there.'

Bullshit. There is no way I am turning up to any drinks organised by Neil.

He then leans in close and begins to whisper in my ear, I almost want to gag from the putrid smell he is producing;

'It's always good to keep me on your side Ryan as you wouldn't want people to find out what you were getting up to with that receptionist on your first day here.'

Ryan 1, Neil 2.

Fucking shit bag of a human being. He's outright blackmailing me and I haven't even done anything wrong. It looks like at this stage, I have no choice but to go along to his stupid drinks night this Saturday. I need to know the lie of the land in this office and see whether people will be Team Ryan or Team Knobhead Neil.

'Raj and Dan won't be coming as apparently they go to Taekwondo on that evening, don't you boys?'

They both nod their heads quickly and go back to pretending to be really absorbed in their computer screens, in the hope this ogre will go back to his cave soon. After a few minutes of Neil grinning like a rat at all three of us, he eventually slimes his way back to his side of the office. I give Raj and Daniel a friendly G'day when he leaves, but they won't even look at me. It is bad enough I am doing my job on the other side of the world in a new environment but it looks like it is going to be made even harder by needing to win over my work colleagues and ensure the slimeball Neil doesn't make me the pariah of the office.

And to top it all off, I've just realised that the 'compulsory' Saturday night drinks is the same night as Ruby's opening night at The Lemon Tree. I need to attend and make a good impression at both of these events but the reality is that I can probably only attend one. Shitty shit shit.

Ryan 1, Neil 3.

Ryan's attempt at a nice life: -3000.

They think it's all over… well it is now.

CHAPTER 13

The delicate petals of the pink peonies feel so soft and comforting. I still can't believe this is happening. I breathe in their scent once more before I add them to the display shelf ready for tonight. I feel incredibly lucky that I, Ruby Samuels, just a normal, okay maybe slightly quirky, twenty-seven year old woman has somehow made something that felt like it could only be a dream into a reality. I have Granddad Shane to thank for making this shop a possibility. As a tribute to him I have ordered some lemon sherbets to go in some of the glass vases at the back of the shop so that people can help themselves to them during the evening. I can just imagine Granddad Shane trying to find the nearest chair and plonking himself in it, muttering about the state of the world whilst he dives into his green knitted cardigan and pulls out the brown paper bag full of his favourite sweets. Despite always being a grumpy sod, I do miss him so.

'Ding Ding.'

The rattle of the shop doorbell shakes me out of my daydreaming and almost makes me break the stems of the peonies I have just put on the display. I hope that Catrina can deal with the customer. I regain my composure and carry on putting the remaining perfectly pink peonies on the shelf next to the white roses. Apparently white roses are the biggest trend in floristry at the moment, well I hope it is anyway as I've ordered a whole load to be delivered throughout the month and if things aren't rosy, then I am definitely going to be feeling the thorns and the bank manager prodding my sides.

The official opening isn't until tonight but the shop was kitted out and all ready to go by Thursday so it seemed silly not to open early, especially as flowers don't tend to last forever. And I am so glad I did as people have been curious enough to walk inside to find out what The Lemon Tree is all about. Although people's responses to a new shop have been mixed, with some being absolutely lovely customers and others goddam rude.

People are curious creatures though and can't help but have a look at a new shop, although I have seen some of the ruder members of the public use the old technique of pretending you are not there as you say hello to them as they walk in. I've seen this avoidance trick before when I worked with Tess. These type of people get scared that you are going to give them the hard sell and will start ramming succulents down their throat if they don't buy anything. They think by sticking their nose in the air and by just ignoring you they won't be approached and can carry on examining every single item of the shop before leaving empty-handed. I can't do the hard sell and I wouldn't do it even if I could, which is why it would be nice to get a general greeting of hello when they walk in, but I suppose it is tough being a philistine in this world.

I'm used to dealing with these types of people but what I am not used to is customers coming into the shop making a grander entrance than Dame Shirley Bassey belting out 'Goldfinger' at the Albert Hall. A woman came in on the first day, dressed in a bright turquoise kaftan with matching eyeshadow, fuchsia pink lipstick, large gold hoop earrings and a perpetually swinging blue plastic carrier bag which was going round and round in her chunky right hand and continually threatened to take out half of my orchid display. She then shrilled at the top of her voice;

'HELLO DARLING, HOW ARE YOU TODAY?'

Her violent entrance also lead to the two customers browsing some purple lavender to become shrinking violets and immediately leave the shop in case this woman would eat them alive, and by the size of this turquoise-clad woman it look like she had already swallowed a whole bus full of school children.

Not only did I lose two potential customers because of the turquoise tank but Catrina and I then had to deal with her continuing theatrics, being her only remaining audience members.

'WELL ISN'T THIS A PRETTY SHOP. AREN'T YOU CLEVER LITTLE GIRLS TO BE RUNNING THIS.'

I could see Catrina's foot tapping as she tried to hold back saying anything to the woman as I give her the eye to reign in her inner Welsh dragon. The last thing I need is someone slagging off the Lemon Tree online, even if they were the antagonising party. I smiled politely at the tank and asked if she needed any help.

She clearly did need help but not the help you would find in a florist. She also presumed I was stone deaf as she continued to shout at me;

'I AM LOOKING FOR A PINK FLOWER TO MATCH MY LIPSTICK. DO YOU HAVE ONE?'

She then puckered her lips towards me like some sort of trout as if this action will help me get a closer look at the shade of lipstick she has on, presuming I am not only deaf but partially blind.

By the luck of the gods, I actually managed to find a pink rose that was a perfect match and show it to her.

'OH NO! WHAT'S THE MATTER WITH YOU GIRL. THAT DOESN'T MATCH AT ALL, YOU MUST NEED YOUR EYES TESTED. FIND ME ANOTHER ONE'.

With her podgy left hand she shooed me away to find another pink flower as she stood still twirling her plastic bag and now threatening my lavender plant display.

I saw Catrina clench her fists and join Laurence in the stock room, I swear I saw steam emanating from her nostrils. That first flower matched perfectly and I know damn well that there is nothing wrong with my eyes, there is just something wrong with this woman's brain.

I spent a whole hour going through every single pink flower in the shop and despite there being several flowers that could have matched her lipstick, it was never the right shade and before I showed her the last of the pink flowers available she then decided to flounce out of the shop shouting;

'I'VE GOT TO GO DARLINGS, I AM A VERY BUSY WOMAN Y'KNOW… PEOPLE NEED ME IN THEIR LIFE. TOODLES.'

Yeah like people need a hole in the head. These people are the absolute worse. They are all show and no action as they are guaranteed not to buy a single thing in the shop. In fact they make you feel as if you owe them a living.

Despite ridiculous time-wasters like the turquoise tank, sales have been high, although many of them were regular customers from my market seller days, who came in and got their regular orders and wished me well with my shop, I also seem to be a hit with my fellow millennials probably due to my social media presence. Laurence is an absolute babe for setting all that up. Fingers crossed they keep making an appearance and help my business grow, I really need to stop with these floral and plant puns in my thinking, it's probably because I am surrounded by everything green and I am rooting for this to work… oh god I did it again.

Catrina, bless her beautiful Welsh heart has been an absolute godsend, dealing with awkward customers, staying longer than the hours I have assigned her and still finding time to fit in her studies and make the best cups of tea ever. If it wasn't for her help there would be no way this shop would be in a fit state to open tonight, let alone a few days beforehand. I just hope I make enough money to keep her on.

'Ruby. Do you have a minute? This bloke wants to talk to you.'

Sounds like another tricky customer, the last thing I need on opening night is someone complaining about my beautiful shop.

'Ruby, this looks bloody fantastic!'

Shit. Bugger. Bugger. One of the thorns from the roses has pierced right through my thumb due to the jolt of having someone so close to me. I get ready to give the idiot a mouthful for being way too close to the shop window, which could have caused a more serious accident, and then as I look up, I decide not to be so rude.

How can I let such a gorgeous man get me angry. I smile bashfully and then, as I try to hide my bleeding thumb behind my back, he places a soft kiss on my left cheek which immediately makes me go bright red.

'So how the hell are ya?' shouts his mate next to him, feeling slightly left out. I quickly give him a hug but immediately place my gaze back at this man.

I can't believe Ryan and Chad are in the shop. I quickly brush myself down with my non-injured hand. Of all the days, they come in today. I really wish I had made more of an effort with my make-up today.

'I just thought I would pop by to see how everything is going and whether you would like us to give you a hand with anything.'

'I thought we were going to the pub…' interjects Chad.

Ryan tries to bat Chad away and pretends he can't hear as he focuses his eyes directly on mine.

'I am a strong willed woman. I am a strong willed woman.' I silently chant to myself over and over in my head. Just when I can picture spending the rest of my life with Laurence, Ryan always makes an appearance to muddy the waters.

'Hey guys, so good to see you,' I say trying to look cool and collected.

'Well we are near enough ready for the opening tonight so there isn't much left to sort out…'

I can hear Catrina deliberately pulling the Sellotape so it makes an extra 'thhhhrummmp' sound whilst wrapping some bouquets, just so she can get involved with what is going on and find out who these two rather good looking men are. Catrina only talks when invited to, but when she is invited she can be the life and soul of the party, unless of course she is with those hideous flatmates of hers.

I do the necessary introductions so that at least everyone knows each other's names.

'How's it going boys?', she says in her dulcet Welsh tones.

'When's you off to the Beach Boys concert then?' she says as she looks them up and down in their bright coloured shirts that are just peeping above their thick woollen winter coats.

I love Catrina and her sense of humour but I am not sure how well a pair of Aussie men will take her broad approach. Ryan looks a bit puzzled but Chad on the other hand…

'The same time as your Country and Western gig,' as Chad looks at the red checked shirt Catrina is wearing underneath her apron.

Catrina lets out a small smile from her bright red lipsticked mouth and does a small flick of her newly styled and cut short brown bob. Is Catrina attempting to flirt with Chad? I've never seen her flirt with anyone like that before but then I haven't known her that long, although she told me once that her flatmates said she would never get a boyfriend unless she loses a few pounds.

Catrina isn't fat anyway, she's a size fourteen for goodness sake. The average U.K size for women is a sixteen and it's not like she's pushing rolls of fat back in her trousers, she's a beautiful woman both inside and out and hopefully she will see that one day and ignore those nasty comments and will find her Prince Charming like I have with Laurence. Despite the current confident aura she is emitting, I can see behind the till that she is squashing her nails into her fist in order to retain her composure.

Although it looks like Chad seems to be interested as well as he is getting closer and closer to her; Ryan says he has been moping around recently due to him not getting over Charlie, so it might do the pair of them the world of good to know that there are other nice single people in the world.

'You don't sound like Ruby, do you come from somewhere else in England?' says Chad.

'Don't be so insulting! I am an out and proud Welsh woman I'll let you know.'

Oh shit, Catrina may have come across a tad aggressive there as Chad has gone bright red and no longer looks like the relaxed surfer dude I remember him as, Catrina's eyes also widen at his sudden change of expression and attempts to pacify the situation;

'It's alright, I didn't expect a tanned and tough Aussie like you to know something as important as the difference between the English and the Welsh so I'll let you off this time... but only the once.'

She winks at him and in return he offers his best schoolboy smile. I want to sit and watch them both all day just to see how things will develop but then I realise Ryan is standing opposite me and has been watching every move I take. I look straight back into his rich green eyes and as our gaze meets, he immediately looks away, moves a step back and then fills the awkward silence between us.

'Honestly Ruby, good on ya for making this place look extraordinary. It shouldn't be a surprise though as I know you are a talented woman.'

I feel my face becoming red again and I am finding it hard to think of how to continue the conversation. I have this sudden urge to touch him, to be closer to him than the safe distance he is currently keeping, the pair of us clearly unsure as to how to act around each other after all that has happened. Can we be friends and forget about those feelings we had for each other? I don't know whether we can.

I mumble a thanks to his compliment and suddenly the need for his touch becomes too much. I outstretch my arms in order to invite him for a friendly hug. That should be okay, just a hug, just a friend embracing a friend for a nice compliment received and to move on from all the things that have happened between us. I mean I've kept a pretty low profile anyway by only sending him business stuff and not texting him all the time. It is he who needs to control himself not I, he is the one who has sought me out not the other way round.

As we embrace, I feel his strong arms around my back and it makes me feel warm and comfortable inside and I don't want him to let go. I am not sure he wants this embrace to end either as he keeps his hands locked around my back.

'What are you doing here?' says a stern voice which makes me immediately let go of Ryan and jump twenty feet away from him as if I had found out he had caught chlamydia from a koala.

Shit it's Laurence. I completely forgot he was at the back of the shop helping get the stock room tidy and ensuring it is health and safety compliant. He even bought himself a fancy tape measure with lasers to accurately measure by the millimetre the exact amount of aisle space we needed to ensure there isn't an accident.

I feel incredibly guilty, yet again letting my feelings of lust cloud my judgement when these delicious feelings of warmth and love should be shared with Laurence not Ryan.

I begin to stutter out a response and look desperately at Ryan to help me out. I can see that his eyes have expanded to twice the size due to Laurence surprising him like that but despite his eyes giving the game away to me, in front of everyone else he remains composed and acts as everything is absolutely fine.

'Hi Laurence, how are ya? I was just congratulating Ruby on this shop of hers. I'm also here to give you a hand if you like in setting up.'

'Yes, well if you want to congratulate her there is a time and a place to do it. This evening at her opening event would be when you along with everyone else should be congratulating her. No need for your help as we are nearly finished anyway.'

Ryan has been caught off guard. He thought going in for the friendly tactic would work with Laurence. Even I'm surprised by Laurence's blunt reply. Although I can't blame him as this is the second time Ryan has made an unplanned appearance in his life.

'Look mate, I'm only trying to look out for a friend, no need to be arsey about it.'

I see a flash of anger rip across Laurence's face and I feel a pit of fear in my stomach that this is not going to end well for any of us.

I try and distract them by asking Ryan whether he is coming tonight. As soon as the words leave my mouth I realise this could make the situation a whole lot worse, but I need to know if he is coming tonight, I want him to come tonight.

Before Ryan can even open his mouth to reply, Laurence steps towards him, pushes his chest out and points out of the window.

'Oh look, here comes a customer. You boys better be going now as we can't have Ruby missing out on any potential sales now can we?'

I turn to look outside and see it is that god awful woman again; the turquoise tank. I want to open my mouth to say that Ryan can stay as the woman is a time waster but I know it is not worth causing any more trouble for mine and Laurence's relationship.

'You're right mate, I don't want Ruby's business to go downhill because some scruffy Aussie like me is distracting her.'

He quickly glances in my direction and gives me a small smile and I feel my insides tumble into pure bliss, despite the fact I really wish I didn't feel like this for him still. Both he and I are crossing a thin line, and I hope Laurence didn't catch that brief moment between us.

'Well it was good to see you mate, maybe let us know next time you want to make an appearance so we can deal with your arrival.'

Laurence is really pissed off and I feel guilty that I am the one responsible for it.

I look over to Chad and Catrina to see if they are witnessing the testosterone match that is going on here and see if they can help referee but they seem oblivious and in their own little world. I see Chad slip something into Catrina's hand and I desperately want to know what it is but Laurence blocks my view again as he tries to usher out both the boys, so we can deal with this customer.

Ryan, knowing he has overstayed his welcome and clearly wanting to leave before he punches something or someone, goes over to Chad and grabs him by the arm.

I try and ask Ryan one more time as he stands in the entrance to leave if he will be there tonight but yet again fate is working against me as the Turquoise Tank has returned and barged right into him.

'WHAT'S THE MATTER WITH YOU BOY.'

He looks extremely embarrassed as his cheeks have flushed a deep crimson and pink spots have appeared on his neck just above his colourful shirt. He quickly mumbles an apology to the woman and, still dragging Chad by the arm, who has his eyes fixed on Catrina, makes a hasty and undignified exit.

'I'VE COME TO LOOK FOR A NICE PINK PEONY, LIKE THE ONE IN THE SHOP WINDOW BUT PINKER...' shouts the Turquoise Tank.

Not again. Please god do not make me do this charade again.

'IS THAT MILDRED...? WHY YES, I THINK IT IS. EXCELLENT... WELL I BETTER BE GOING GIRLS, I NEED MILDRED TO HELP ME WITH MY PETITION TO INSTALL MORE SPEED BUMPS IN THE AREA. TOODLES.'

My prayers have been answered and with a large bang of the door, which I am surprised is still attached to its hinges, she disappears. I don't know who the hell Mildred is but I already feel sorry for her. I should have felt a sense of relief that she had left but there was still a sense of awkwardness in the shop with what happened before.

Thankfully Catrina is always good at breaking the silence.

'Chad's a right hottie Ruby. It must be some sort of joke.'

I try to ask her what would be a joke but Laurence has decided to swing into action by grabbing my hand and pushing me slightly back on to his other arm in order to place a full kiss on my mouth right in the middle of the shop and in front of Catrina, not really very professional and rather hypocritical considering what happened. I delicately try to pull away whilst not trying to offend Laurence but thankfully Catrina comes to the rescue again.

'Look you bloody lovebirds, don't forget there is someone else in this shop other than yourselves. We need to get cracking with getting this shop in tip top condition for opening night.'

Catrina then throws a roll of Sellotape in our direction which ends up bouncing right off the top of Laurence's forehead and he makes a loud 'Ow' sound and begins to rub his forehead as he tries to find the Sellotape that has now rolled out of sight on the shop floor.

I gaze for a moment out of the shop window in the hope that I could see Ryan down the end of the high street but it is too late he has already gone; I really do hope he turns up tonight. I know I am playing with fire, but maybe the more I see him the more I can extinguish the flame.

'Oi Ruby,' bellows Catrina, 'didn't you hear me? we need to get some more of these bouquets ready for tonight. We need to make sure this opening event of yours is really special.'

We do indeed and I know what would make it even more special…

CHAPTER 14

And still it seems I am tormented by love. Yet again I lost out on the chance to explain myself to Ruby and tell her why I can no longer go to her opening night. I could send her a text I suppose, but I don't know what to say without coming off like a dick and looking like I am not interested. I had thought about ringing her as well but I don't want her to answer it when her long-haired lover is around as it will put me on edge and I know that Ruby and I won't be able to talk freely.

Just when I feel like I might be getting a little closer to Ruby, someone puts a hurdle in my way to prevent us reuniting.

I really can't give her radio silence though, as she will think I really don't care about her and just want to get into her knickers like I did when I first met her. Maybe I will send her a text later, or maybe I can get away with having just the one pint with Knobhead Neil and can turn up to her event later. Yes, that could be a plan. I could both save my job and prevent Ruby thinking I am the biggest anus of Australia.

I wish Chad was coming with me tonight but he has his first bar shift tonight at some cabaret place called 'Pink Pussycats'. It doesn't sound like the type of bar Chad would drink in but he seems pretty happy that he finally has a job and he gets to wear his favourite loud tropical Hawaiian shirts. If he was here, I could tell him my plan and he would be able to tell Knobhead Neil to back off like he did that ranga kid at the pool when we were little, and we can then both finally start enjoying life in London. Although Chad is still acting weird, after the whole 'Matilda-gate' situation he no longer seems to be interested in chasing anything with two legs, in fact he doesn't even look at any women even though there have been quite a few eyeing him up recently; instead he has been asking me about Wales. No idea why, maybe he wants to be a sheep farmer or something. It wouldn't surprise me with Chad.

I finally reach Clapham Junction tube station and pull my jumper closer to my nose in order to keep me warm on this winter's night. I know people said England was cold but the reality is that it is fucking freezing. It feels like I am currently wearing the whole of my wardrobe and I still can't feel my toes. It's days like today that I want to go home and soak up the Sydney sunshine as the only thing that is bringing me any warmth here is the thought of possibly reuniting with Ruby. Yet the likelihood of us getting together is getting slimmer and slimmer and so is my ability to ward off frostbite.

I quickly walk out of the station and immediately spot 'The Gardeners Arms', a pub that looks like a dream meeting place for the drug addled, psychotics and serial killers. It sends a shiver down my spine unrelated to the cold. It is probably the grottiest pub I have seen in my time here but I shouldn't be surprised as Knobhead's Neil's standards of taste are so low they go beyond the gutter. Before I even get near to the pub door I hear an awful sound;

'Maaaatttteeee… how's it going?'

Talk of the devil and he shall appear. Just looking at him turns my stomach, he has a beer in one hand and a cigarette balancing out of his mouth full of tombstones. It is clear he is losing his hair and, rather than doing what any self-respecting bloke would do and shave it off, he has decided to comb over his thinning greasy hair just enough to cover the crow's nest at the back. No wonder he doesn't want to rush back to Australia, as despite being a citizen of the country, customs would probably try and dispose of him as a bio-hazard. I had totally forgotten how he can make you feel embarrassed and at risk of losing your job due to him putting you in a compromising position. No wonder those guys at the office looked like they shit themselves and created fictitious hobbies in order to avoid spending time with him. I should have been quicker with an excuse, although knowing me I probably would've said something like I am off to origami class or something else just as lame. And then I really would be destroyed by Neil whilst everyone else in the office stays silent as I become the sacrificial lamb.

As I've been sizing up this disgusting beast, I realise that I haven't yet responded to his greeting.

'What's the matter with ya mate? Worried that I will show you up because I'm better looking than ya and get all the girls,' he smirks as he flicks his cigarette ash in the air which almost lands in someone's hair.

Show me up yes. Because you are better looking than me, no. The rats that run along the tube tunnels are more attractive than he is.

I just grin at him, give him a pat on the shoulder and try and steer him towards the inside of the pub so I can get a drink and then go.

Unfortunately, he grabs my shoulder in return, and as he does so, he manages to spill some of the beer on my coat sleeve. For fuck's sake this coat is from Armani as well. And so much for receiving an apology from Neil, instead he thinks I have lost my hearing rather than a designer coat and begins shouting down my ear;

120

'MATE, JUST WAIT A SEC. I WANT TO SHOW YOU THE SEXY GIRLS WE WILL BE HANGING OUT WITH TONIGHT.'

I look up to the night sky and wonder if some lightning can just strike me down now, just a light burn or some sort of minor injury that lands me in A&E, as I have a feeling it would be a better night out than the one I am going to have with Neil and these 'sexy girls'. I really hope they are not prostitutes, I have never used one, never needed one and never more than now want to be seen with one. If Ruby finds out that I spent the evening sat next to one in the pub instead of going to her opening night, our relationship that hasn't even restarted will be over.

Neil then pushes my back again so I am flung forward into the busy pub door and towards the bar, so much for seeing these 'sexy girls' first. As he continues to push me I try to apologise to all the people who I am bulldozing straight into. I don't even have to open my mouth and already Neil is ensuring that everyone in the pub hates me.

As I get shunted to the bar and feel my blood pressure hit the roof, I turn to confront Neil in order to tell him to back off and prove that I do in fact have a back bone. As I do so he has already leaned over the bar and whistled at the bar maid to get her attention. If that was me I would be seriously annoyed or pretend I am deaf, yet somehow, rather than telling him to 'piss off' and wait his turn like the rest of the customers in the pub, she goes straight to him in order to hear what he has to say. He may be the biggus dickus of the world but his tactics clearly work as he always seems to get what he wants.

'Hey love, can you get us two large glasses of chardonnay, a large whiskey and a pint of Carlsberg.'

'RYAN, WHAT DO YOU WANT?' he shouts loudly in my ear

despite the fact I am next to him. The pub is busy but it isn't the noisiest of places, if people weren't staring after my bulldozer impression, they certainly are now. On the plus side at least Neil will be buying me a drink.

'I'll have a Carlsberg as well please Neil.'

'Ooooh please Neil, you've definitely turned into an uptight Pommie haven't you? Get him a Carlsberg as well then love, it might loosen him up a bit.'

He winks at the barmaid but she just responds with a blank stare, she is probably used to dealing with customers like Neil and knows the best response is no response. As she begins to pour out the drinks and I think of a way to escape this hell, Neil grins another grimy tombstone smile at me and then walks away from the bar.

'That will be thirty five pounds then please,' she says as she puts the last pint down in front of me with a large thud. She puts her hand out for me to pay up. I am left dumbfounded as to what has just happened but the barmaid doesn't care as long as someone pays so she repeats the request again but even slower ensuring I have no way out of paying or saying I misheard her.

'Thaaaatttt is thhhhirrrrtttttyyyyy fiiiiivvveee pooouuuunnnddss.'

I hand over my card and hope that my pay from the first week of work is in my account otherwise tonight is going to be even more awkward. I punch my pin into the machine and thankfully it returns a green tick knowing I am safe as long as Neil doesn't fool me into buying the whole pub this evening. I can hear Neil laughing evilly just a few metres behind me, pleased with himself that he has tricked me before I even take a sip of my beer.

'Oi mate, we are just in the corner over there, do hurry up, we're parched.' Again the whole bar is looking at me and I do my best to try and prove through sign language in the hope that people know I am actually here against my will.

I take the tray of drinks and carry them as carefully as I can towards Neil and his fellow cretins.

'If you don't hurry up mate, you'll be buying the rounds for the rest of the night as well.'

Fuck you Neil. Fuck you. I am half tempted to throw his drink over him but it seems I am still trying to find my testicles and I don't want him to make my life hell at work, plus I paid a lot of money for those drinks so it would be a shame to waste it on someone like Neil. I worked very hard to get to where I am as an accountant and intend to be the top of my game both here and back home. I don't need bastards like him ruin my chances.

As I carefully place the tray of drinks on the table, I get the chance to take in these 'sexy ladies' that I presume Neil has been referring to. They don't appear to be prostitutes thank god, although they might as well be sitting in their underwear with a red light on due to the way they are dressed. I recognise the peroxide blonde on the left immediately as Karen from Reception and using my refined Sherlock Holmes skills I presume the women with the burgundy rinse next to her is her friend.

'Hiya Ryan, so good that you can join us. Neil is such a laugh but when there's two girls and just one boy it can be a bit awkward if you know what I mean. HAHAHAHA.'

Christ almighty, Karen laughs like a deranged crow and with her thick-kohl rimmed eyes and beak of a nose she looks like one too, I have a feeling she will be doing her best with her dimwit mate of hers to peck both my eyes out before the night comes to an end.

'I told you ladies, I am down for a threesome if you are,' grins Neil.

I feel the bile begin to rise up in my throat again and decide to take a swig of my beer in the hope it will put me at ease amongst these circus animals. Although I remember a time when I said something similar to Ruby when I first meet her, the flashback immediately makes me cringe inside.

'Ooooh Neil you can be so naughty sometimes,' squeals Karen in response as she gives the top of Neil's left thigh a big squeeze whilst simultaneously rearranging her skirt in order to give him an eyeful.

'This is my friend Kirsten by the way,' she says dismissively with her eyes still glued to Mr Knobhead, it is clear that Neil is her main target here. I am more than happy for her, but that doesn't mean I want her friend as company or even god forbid a bedfellow, I'd rather gouge my own eyes out.

'Pleased to meet you Ryan.'

She deliberately leans over to shake my hand so I can get a full view of her assets, which really aren't much to look at. It's enough to put me off my beer. She moves closer to my side of the table and, due to the fact I am shoved into the corner, it appears I have no escape from this monstrous woman as she sits here, with red lipstick already smeared across her cheek, wearing a denim mini skirt and low cut emerald green top. She is getting closer and closer to squashing me to death. She also appears to have eaten some cheese and onion crisps as her breath is horrendous, it's so bad in fact I have to put my hand over my nose, which she doesn't even register as her eyes seems to be squarely fixed on my crotch. It's times like this I really wish I didn't have a penis.

The only positive I can take from these two is that they are not prostitutes and I am less likely to get in trouble with the law or Ruby if she ever finds out about tonight.

As the evening continues, my tolerance rapidly decreases and I keep my answers monosyllabic and avoid starting conversations, but the others don't seem to care. or are already so drunk they don't notice I am not interested in them or their shitty inappropriate jokes. It is only the continual back slaps that I get from Neil that ensure they are keeping me in the group, meaning I can't escape. I also appeared to have paid for another 3 rounds which is much more than the one measly round Neil has bought.

I look up at the clock and see that it is 10:00pm already. I need to leave soon in order to get to Ruby's opening before it ends at 11:00 pm. I decide to send her a good luck text to show her that I am thinking about her and that I am hoping to turn up later, if I can get away from Kirsten and her podgy fingers that are slowly trying to creep up my leg. I continually try to swat her hand away as if I am trying to exterminate a fly, yet she still doesn't get the message and tries to rub rather than creep her way up. I try and move my legs away from her but as space is limited there isn't much I can do.

But first I need to send this text. I get out my phone and begin to compose a message.

'And what do you think you're doing…' bellows Neil.

He grabs the phone straight from my hands and waves it above his head. I abruptly stand up in order to grab it from his hands and almost tip over the table and rip off Kirsten's hand. That will teach her for gluing her hand to my leg.

'Give it back Neil.' I say both firmly and angrily. Finally I appear to be growing a pair of balls.

'Oooooohhhhh Ryan is getting his little knickers in a twist. Now let's see who he thought was more interesting to text than enjoying a night out with his mates..'

I lunge forward again but still Neil manages to hold on to my phone whilst I disrupt the table again, this time spilling Karen's glass of wine across her skirt which makes her yelp like a little terrier dog. I am trapped. Despite leaning over the table to try and push it I can't move as Neil's fat gut keeps the table in place. He is now scrolling through my phone and laughing manically as he thinks of the next evil plan he wants to unleash against me.

'Looks like you're gonna have to get another round in now you've spilt Karen's drink… So whose this Ruby girl then?'

'None of your business.'

I want to murder him right here and right now. He has gone way too far. He can ridicule me all he likes but I do not want him to have anything to do with Ruby.

'Well it's my business now I have your phone. Maybe I should send this Ruby a message.'

'Don't you dare.'

'Looks like this chick means something to you. You know what I think a picture will be a better than a text message.'

My heart is hammering and I can feel the blood vessels in my neck constrict and my fists begin to clench.

Neil gets up from his chair and walks over to where I am trapped in the corner seat next to Kirsten and then grabs hold of the back of my head, causing me to emulate Scrappy Doo as I try to grab my phone back. He then pushes my head straight into Kirsten's heaving cleavage and before I have a chance to get myself out and far away from her sweaty chest as humanly possible, I hear a click and then in the corner of my eye see a flash. And Kirsten appears to have found this hilarious. To be honest it's probably the closest a male in his late twenties has touched her in a very long time.

'What a picture! I think your friend will love to see this.'

Red mist is beginning to descend in front of my eyes and I have a feeling all hell is about to break lose in a few seconds.

'GIVE IT BACK!!!'

The whole pub is looking at us now and rather than making Neil back down this in fact encourages him as he hits the send button and places the phone in his front pocket at the top of his shirt with a satisfied smug look on his face.

'No, you can get it back at the end of the night when you've stopped being such a sourpuss.'

I raise my fist and think better of it. Neil wants the drama for the office gossip and to get me out of my job. He knows I am good at what I do and he would love to get me fired due to a punch-up. I am a big threat to him in the workplace as I am much better at accountancy than he is. This is why he plays these games, it's frustrating that it has only taken me until now to realise that I could have had the upper hand in these situations if I just ignored him and his petty games.

I sit back down in the corner and let Neil think he has won. He may have won the battle but he hasn't won the war. Thankfully when I do sit down Kirsten has backed right off and appears to be making eyes at the overweight skinhead in his fifties at the bar. His beer goggles are directly looking at her as well, it looks like those two are sorted for the evening and my genitals are now safe from anymore gropey hands this evening.

I try to spend the next few hours or so being polite and not acting pissed off in order to show Neil that he has not and will not break me. Besides it's too late anyway the damage is done.

At around 2am Kirsten appears to be giving the guy at the bar mouth to mouth and Karen is sucking on Neil's neck like some octopus feeding on its prey. And rather surprisingly it appears Neil would actually like to go home and have sex with Karen than in the pub despite them near enough dry humping each other to the amusement of everyone else in the pub whilst I sit here like a tool, waiting for my phone. Finally, he decides to take the phone out of his pocket and slide it across the table meaning I now have a scratched screen as well as a broken heart. Neil then briefly comes up for air;

'Here you go mate, some of us have business to attend to if you know what I mean wink wink nudge nudge.'

I shouldn't have come at all tonight, I should've gone straight to Ruby's opening night but just recently I appear to like making things hard for myself. I immediately send Ruby a text to tell her that picture isn't what it seems but I know it is too late. It's probably for the best, she has a chance at love with Laurence I can't take that away from her and hurt her anymore than I already have, maybe it is the Universe's way of telling me to move on.

I push the pub entrance door open and allow the cold winter air to fill my lungs until they hurt from the iciness and begin my journey back to the apartment. I should have been a man and told Neil to fuck off, he has no right to embarrass or coerce anyone in the office to do as he says. My track record at work would be enough to prove that anything Neil accuses me of is clearly a pack of lies, if only I had the sense to realise this earlier. It's time to stand up for myself and get what I want not just in work but in life too. Neil has lost my chance in love and I will ensure that he nor anyone else will ever get in the way of

128

someone I love again, that's if I ever get the chance to love again...

CHAPTER 15

Where is he? I really thought he would be here tonight. This is meant to be one of the most significant nights of my life, finally getting to open my own floristry shop and here I am wondering whether a guy, who is not my boyfriend will decide to turn up.

Despite this being my opening night, I have managed to get the job of standing at the front door greeting everyone who comes in and offering them a glass of champagne from the big metal tray I currently have balancing on my forearms. Every time I try to put the tray down and mingle with the crowd to discuss my floristry work, I get someone wanting to take a glass of champagne from me. In fact there is one woman who has come up to my tray three times in the last half an hour, and every time she does so, she pretends that it's her first glass despite looking more dishevelled each time.

'Oooh you have champagne, how splendid. I will only have the one glass. I don't like to be greedy.'

This opening night was for family, friends, and friends of friends; not opportunistic passers-by. I'm pretty sure this woman knows no one other than Mr. Bollinger and at the rate everyone is acquainting themselves with him it won't be long until he disappears too, so let's see how long she stays around then. Although now that she has just spotted Mr. Kipling she might be here a little bit longer.

Despite people clicking their fingers and demanding that I provide them with a drink, even from my own mother, it appears that things are going very well on the opening night. It may be a cold winter evening but the place is packed and every time I look over at Catrina she is serving yet another customer.

I am wondering if this busyness is down to my mother who is demanding anyone in her sight to buy something from the shop to support her 'baby girl'. Excruciatingly embarrassing but it does keep the till ringing and besides I should've known better to invite my mother to an event that serves alcohol. I can't complain too much and the joy of seeing so many people buy flowers makes me feel happy but it seems not happy enough to stop the constant thoughts in my head of Ryan.

I need to get a grip. Ryan has caused too much trouble and distraction already, sure he wrote me a heartfelt letter but it has been Laurence who has been my rock. He has been here from the start, offering help and advice where he can. It should only be him I am thinking of especially as I have been such a lousy girlfriend recently. The Lemon Tree has taken up all my free time and every time I have promised to cook dinner for Laurence, it ended in me seeking the help of Ronald McDonald or Colonel Sanders to provide us with something to eat, not the best options for a veggie boyfriend.

Laurence just laughs it off and says that he knows that I am busy and the shop is the most important thing right now but I do feel exceptionally guilty, especially as he cooks the most delicious meals from scratch and often follows up the gut-pleasing meal with a foot rub too.

And let me tell you, he is a very brave man to touch my feet after a hard day running around this shop. The smell that is released from my tootsies when they are out of my shoes, could be classed as a dangerous chemical weapon. Either Laurence is completely nose blind or he has managed to peg his nostrils without me seeing but that really is dedication. Even my dad has joked that the best way to distinguish Martha and I as twins would be to smell our feet. Although if anyone did try that I doubt they would be able to get up again.

I feel a pinch on my arm to wake me up from my toe-ridden thoughts and it almost makes me drop the tray of champagne on the floor. The ninja pincher is Laurence and he is looking rather dashing this evening with a blue velvet jacket and fitted white shirt, it is a shame his hair still looks a bit weird but I am sure it will either grow on me in the next few months or he will get bored of this look and get a proper haircut. Hopefully the latter as it will stop my dad calling him 'Mop A Top'.

'Hey Babe, do you mind if I just say a couple of words to the guests about all your hard work.'

I agree to it, knowing it will take the pressure off of me needing to say anything tonight. I do love talking to people but only in small groups not in crowded situations like this, it makes me feel really nervous and on the urge of an anxiety attack. My hands are already damp and feel as if they are sliding off the tray just at the thought of being the centre of attention.

Yet again, Laurence is my saviour. However, the devil is still tapping me on the shoulder as I finally manage to put the champagne tray down and delve into the front of my apron pocket to access my phone.

I have 0 messages. God damn it Ryan, just send me something and then I can actually focus on enjoying tonight.

Suddenly Laurence taps loudly on his champagne flute, to a point where I wonder whether it will smash into a thousand pieces. Those glasses weren't cheap so I really hope they will sustain the damage.

I then see Dad nudge his elbow into Mum's side and mumble;

'Brace yourself Sue, Mop A Top is about to speak.'

Mum just brushes his elbow away and lets out a 'Pffft' noise in the belief that Laurence will give a good speech and make her daughter shine.

'Thank you all for coming to the Lemon Tree this evening, it is a pleasure to have you here and see so many of you buy lots of flowers and plants from this wonderful shop…'

A good solid start by Laurence, I have a feeling he may just pull this out of the bag for me.

'…she has worked many tireless hours and has probably eaten her body weight in chocolate to get to this stage…'

Okay this isn't quite the turn I was hoping to take but still okay so far unless of course he is trying to insinuate that I am fat.

'…there have been many pricks she has dealt with in getting here, and I am not just talking about the ones from the thorns on the roses but nevertheless she has come out the other end smelling like one of her beautiful bouquets…'

Abort. Abort. This is now going dreadfully, that joke really did not work as only about 3 people in the audience laughed, the rest are staring at the ground in embarrassment.

…I know that Ruby is quite shy but please go and say hello and ask her any questions you may have on floristry as I know she will be able to help tidy up your lady garden at any time. So let's give her a round of applause.'

My life as a credible florist is now officially over. He stands there looking confused as to why no one is clapping and how a few people have had to suppress their giggles, the worst thing is I don't even think he meant the last part of the speech to be a joke.

My Mum's eyes are on stalks and I can see she is already trying to work out how to resolve this situation.

Laurence then heads straight over to my direction so I dart swiftly in the opposite direction, pretending to be busy, in order to prevent me saying something that I will later regret.

If only Ryan was here, he knows how to charm people, he would've done a better speech than Laurence. I tell myself to stop it. Stop thinking about him. Ryan isn't here and he clearly doesn't like me as much as I think, I have been incredibly vain and self-indulgent and need to get out in the world and stand on my own two feet like a true modern woman would do. Although I might just hide behind these lilies for a bit to allow my red and embarrassed face to calm down.

Shit. Mother has seen me and drags me by the arm as if she would a screaming toddler and places me right in the middle of her book club friends.

'Despite that idiot of a boyfriend my daughter has, she really has some great skill when it comes to arranging flowers. Don't you think ladies?'

My mother is not a lady to be messed with when she gets serious and it is clear that the ladies of her book club feel the same way as they all nod in unison in case they get breathed on by the crazy mother dragon.

One of the book club members who appears to be a thin middle-aged woman with a slight squint in her eye decides to take the risk of saying something about the flowers. Maybe the fact she has a squint means she doesn't see the full effect of the 'mother dragon'.

'Oh yes, the Spring collection you have created in the shop window is really quite something, I feel like it really reflects the season. It is very good work.'

Mother feels satisfied with this answer as she crosses her arms, leans forward and says to the rest of the trembling group;

'See I told you I had a clever daughter.'

Again they all nod in unison and look directly at my mother instead of me to ensure that they will live another day with all their limbs intact.

Thankfully Mum gets distracted by someone who is in her aerobics class, in fact the woman looks like Jane Fonda, if Jane Fonda took a whole load of acid and rolled around in a forest. Her eyelids are painted bright green, her lipstick is a shocking pink and her short straw-yellow hair is going in all sorts of directions, not to mention she is wearing a leopard bodysuit and bright pink leggings. She is also precariously waving around a bunch of gladioli around her head and I am hoping that she has paid for those already as every time she swings them a petal seems to come astray meaning they will just be stalks by the end of the night and even the most naïve of customers are unlikely to want to buy some green stalks to decorate their house with.

I look around for Dad and wonder whether he wants to add further to my embarrassment tonight and see that it is already too late as he is currently video calling Martha in Australia so he can show her the shop. He spots me looking and they both stick their tongue out at me simultaneously. Sometimes I wonder whether it is too late to get adopted.

I then feel a buzz in my apron and I sneak off to a quiet part of the shop. As I hide back behind the lilies, I pull my phone out completely from the apron pocket to see the message. It's from Ryan. My heart is beating so quickly I wonder whether it will lift itself up into my throat. I quickly open the message to see what he has to say. He says nothing. It is just a picture of him nuzzling two women who look like mutton dressed as lamb. And there I was thinking he had changed but yet again he appears to be up to his old tricks again of being a dirty and deceiving player. Why would he send me a picture like that? Did he think it was funny? Did he think it would make me jealous?

This night was meant to be one of the best nights of my life, a turning point in how my life as a fully-fledged adult is going but after Ryan's picture and Laurence's speech I feel alone and in need of something to make this night less of a mare. I feel a soft pink hand reach through the lilies and place itself on top of my hand, I look through the leaves and see it is Catrina. I haven't had a chance to speak to her all evening but every-time I have looked over at her, she has been working her absolute socks off ensuring that people are served at the till and answering any requests they may have. An absolute angel and a sign that it is important to keep positive and optimistic about tonight even if it is just for her as she has put in so much effort helping me get this shop off the ground.

'Here' she says passing me a glass of champagne through the lilies with her other hand.

My first drink of the evening.

'I think you need and deserve this.'

I obligingly take the glass, come out of my hiding place and get ready to face the rest of the world again and so I can properly toast with Catrina without a bunch of greenery up my nose. Catrina lifts her glass and gives the best speech of the evening;

136

'Cheers Ruby, no more hiding in the bushes, here's to independent women making their mark on the world.'

'Cheers indeed.'

CHAPTER 16

'What a night,' I mutter to myself as I get into the apartment lift. This was something I used to say when I had got laid by some hot chick or when I had got absolutely smashed with Chad on a night out but tonight this phrase takes on a new meaning. I never want a night like that again, my jaw is still jammed shut from all the tension and frustration this evening.

I feel so mentally and physically exhausted and cannot wait to get back into my own bed, on my own without any more drama. The closer I get to 30 the more I feel like an old man, the days of being the 'top party bloke' are well and truly over.

As I get closer to the door of the apartment and closer to finally collapsing in my bed to end this horrific evening, one of the only positives of tonight is that I was out so late it is past Uncle Terry's curfew. As I get the apartment keys out of my pocket I notice that there is something hanging on the door handle.

It looks like a pair of ladies fishnet tights. There is no way I will be able to get Chad out of this mess now. It's bad enough that I am sneaking in late let alone him having a girl back here again. Fuck me, this night just gets worse and worse.

I take a deep breath and wonder if there is anything else God wants to bring my way tonight to make it the worst night ever in the life of Ryan Crichton. The door being unlocked, pushes freely open allowing loud music to echo into the communal hallway. I would have thought if Uncle Terry was in he would have given Chad his marching orders but I can't hear any commotion, maybe he has gone on a nocturnal walk or maybe he has just collapsed at the shock of Chad's behaviour.

I take a deep breath and prepare myself for the worst and push the door fully open. I can't believe what I am seeing. I rub my eyes just to make sure and look again. Nope, what I am seeing in front of me is definitely real and will probably be etched on my mind forever.

In the middle of the living room is Chad with Uncle Terry dancing around to 'Material Girl' by Madonna. Chad is dressed in his usual uniform of camel coloured shorts and a bold print Hawaiian shirt but Uncle Terry, well I can't quite believe what he has on. He is wearing a short black skirt, sky-high red patent heels, a silky red bodice and his face is covered in a thick layer of make-up.

Well so much for me thinking he needed the nickname 'Tensed Up Terry', in fact 'Tarty Theresa' might be a better name for him. Now I can see why my Mum said Uncle Terry was so much fun. And it also goes some way to explains why he was imposing such weird curfew rules. He probably thought Chad and I would be weird about him going out on the weekends dressed as a woman. I mean it is strange to see my Uncle parading around in skimpy women's clothing but I have no problem with it, I used to love watching the Mardi Gras in Sydney and with the friends my Mum has, weird behaviour has become the norm for me. In fact the only shocking thing about it all is Chad and Uncle Terry's dreadful singing, it makes listening to the two neighbourhood cats scratching each other's eyes out a more appealing choice to listen to.

They really are getting into the swing of things as well, Uncle

Terry has grabbed the TV remote, which Chad also grabs as they sing into it like a microphone both swaying together and trying their best not to fall on the floor.

'BECAUSE WE ARE LIVING IN A MATERIAL WORLD AND I AM A MATER-'

They both stop mid-shout as they realise I am standing there staring at them in disbelief.

Chad looks at me boss-eyed and drunkenly points in my direction;

'Brrrooooo. It is so good to seeee you. Your Uncle T... your Uncle T... hic... came to my bar and despite him being mad at me for about 20 seconds for seeing him... I think it was 20 seconds or maybe it was longer maybe it was like 25 seconds instead... but anyway Uncle T and his friends are just the coolest. See his not as much as a boring fart as we thought...'

I think it is time for Chad to shut up now before he makes things worse.

Chad then suddenly goes quiet but then he begins to stumble in my direction. I think he might be trying to give me a hug but he takes a sharp right towards the plant pot in the corner of the room and empties the contents of his stomach.

All the while Uncle Terry just stands there bright red with embarrassment, unable to look me in the eye as he desperately uses his hands to cover up his hairy chest that is poking out of his tight red bodice. I just can't handle any more of this night, I need to go to bed. I say nothing to the pair of them and just walk straight to my room.

As I firmly close the bedroom door behind me I slump to the floor to take a moment to breathe and then I let out a huge roaring and cathartic laugh. What a day it has been today, and as I let the craziness of the day wash over me I think of Ruby again, the thought makes my laughter stop and my stomach hurt.

It really is time to get some sleep now, I need to have a clear head for tomorrow when I am going to finally work out what I really want from life.

CHAPTER 17

I can hardly breathe. That will teach me to get a dress in a size twelve instead of a fourteen. I had thought running around the shop had made me lose weight, especially when people kept telling me I looked slimmer.

I was hoping to walk into the pub this evening feeling like a Hollywood goddess in this purple pencil dress but the reality is I am going to look like a Z-list celebrity who enjoys flashing her knickers to the paparazzi and that is not the impression I want to give my friends or Ryan. Yep, that's right I invited Ryan to my birthday gathering. I'm still pissed off he couldn't make my opening night and I still think he is a player despite his 'innocent explanation' of that photo but there's something that is still niggling inside, a connection that cannot be explained.

As I desperately try to yank the dress over my hips I look at the label on the purple pencil dress and realise it's a size eight. I am surprised I could even manage to get one leg into this let alone half of my body. The night of all nights; my birthday night, I manage to pick up the wrong sized dress.

I tear off the dress in frustration, and stamp on it to really show the dress who is boss and yank open the wooden doors of my wardrobe. I then stop and look back at the dress in the hope I didn't cause too much damage as I need to return it. I carefully pick the dress up, fold it and place it on my bed before letting out a large sigh at the textile jungle that is inside my wardrobe.

I beginning flinging hangers out of the wardrobe scrabbling through dense cloth before finally coming face to face with the lioness. I had completely forgotten about this dress. It screamed sexy and beautiful when I viewed it online but when I received it in the post the next day the self-conscious alarm screamed so loud in my head I stuffed it straight to the back of the wardrobe.

'Now is the time to take risks'; screams the voice at the back of my head again. I've taken too many risks lately. 'But they've made you happier,' says the voice stronger and louder. I slip the red silky dress off the hanger and place it over my head and enjoy the soft smooth feel of it as it cascades down to my legs, automatically I do a twirl before looking at myself in the mirror.

I immediately put my hand up to my chest, aware there is more on show than normal. And then the self-conscious alarm rings again. But the voice is louder; 'Tonight is not about being safe, it's about being out there, taking a risk and enjoying still being in your twenties.'

I remain strong and begin to find some suitable pieces of jewellery to add to my dress. I choose my gold elephant necklace, a gift from Martha when she went on her gap year to India. It was so lovely to video call her this morning from Australia. Mum and Dad even made her 'virtually' blow out the candles on our chocolate birthday cake. It's days like today that I really miss Martha. My other half. My twin.

Suddenly I hear the familiar echo of 'Ding Dong Merrily on High…' up the stairs and then Dad shouting;

'Mop A Top is at the door!'

I hastily put down the gold hoop earring I was about to put in my ear and run down the stairs. When I reach the bottom, I give Dad a look which tells him that calling Laurence a 'Mop A Top' is not acceptable. In return he just smiles and pats me on the shoulder before heading to the kitchen to join Mum but as he does so he suddenly realises what his little daughter is wearing out this evening;

'You look nice sweetheart, although make sure to wear a coat tonight as you don't want to catch a cold.'

I open the door to Laurence and despite the wait outside he greets me with a big grin and a small cardboard box with the words; 'For the Birthday Girl' scribbled on the side with biro. Presentation isn't really Laurence's forte but you have to give him top marks for at least trying.

'WOW! You look absolutely gorgeous Ruby, give us a twirl!'

I obligingly carry out his request despite feeling a bit silly and knowing my cheeks have now gone the same colour as my dress.

'I was wondering whether it was too much. I've never worn anything like this before,' I say feeling more and more self-conscious.

'Maybe you're right. It's probably best you change as I don't want every man ogling my girlfriend this evening wishing she was with them.'

I look at astonishment at Laurence's face, completely dead pan and then suddenly he cracks up laughing.

'I'm only joking Ruby, wear it you look beautiful, and as to other men, I will give them the death stare and that should warn them off.'

He then finishes his sentence with a wink and I breathe a sigh of relief. Let's hope he is this relaxed if Ryan turns up tonight.

'Are you going to let me in or are you going to make me wait outside with this box until my arms drop off.'

'Sorry Ry… Laurence. Of course, come in, I'd be a pretty awful girlfriend if I made you stand outside all evening.'

Shit. I hope he didn't notice that slight slip of the tongue there.

'Well I think if you did that, you'd find at the end of the evening, I would have got pneumonia and you would have got a text saying you're dumped.'

I give him my best sad face and in return he pushes the box in my hands and plants a soft kiss on my cheek as he steps into the doorway.

'I am really excited for you to open your presents. I am sure you will love them.'

We wander through to the lounge and I place the box on to the middle of the floor, sitting in front of it crossed leg, with Laurence sitting opposite, his legs outstretched around the box and a really cheeky grin on his face. And then I realise why, sitting crossed-leg in this dress has meant I have shown the whole world my knickers, so much for avoiding looking like a Z-list celebrity.

I slowly open the box, knowing it is driving him mad that I am taking my time, we both look each other and let out a small laugh. As I look into the box, I see that there are three wrapped gifts in the box. The wrapping is neat, although the pattern on the paper is made up of big Santa Claus faces.

'You do know it's June this month, not December?'

His face reddens and he puts his hand behind his neck as if to deal with an imaginary scratch.

'Yeah, sorry about that, it was the only wrapping paper I could find at my Mum's house. It was that or the wrapping paper which says 'Happy Birthday Son' on it, so I thought this was the better option. Plus its red, like your name and that gorgeous dress you are wearing.'

I just roll my eyes and laugh, happy that he had made some sort of effort in wrapping them.

'Open that one first.'

Like an eager child he points to the rectangular shaped present in the left hand corner of the box. Too big to hold a ring in but just the type of box that could hold a bracelet or maybe even a necklace. I had been hinting to him recently that I would really like a charm bracelet.

I delicately unwrap it as I feel my fingers tingle with excitement. Once unwrapped, excitement quickly turns to confusion. Why would he get me this? Why would I want a red USB charger for a mobile phone. I take a breath so as to prepare my best fake 'that's wonderful face' to prevent disappointment.

As I look up at him, he gives his explanation as to why an earth he bought me this practical gift.

'Seeing as you are always borrowing my charger, I thought I would get you your own. Plus its red so it will be easy to identify that it's yours.'

Enough with the red theme already, I know my name is Ruby but that doesn't mean I need everything in my sight to be red. I try my hardest not to be ungrateful as it was nice of him to at least buy me something. Although I do hope the next two gifts

146

are at least slightly better.

'This one is next', he says as he thrusts an oval shaped package in my hand. Now this looks more like it. The shape itself is of interest, and I know most things tech related don't tend to come in oval shaped boxes.

I open it up and discover it is a make-up set that mainly consists of dark eyeshadows and dark purple lipsticks. I turn the oval box over and see that it says the make-up is designed for those with dark haired and olive skin complexions; two things I don't have. I would love to have dark hair and olive skin but unfortunately I have blonde curly hair and skin so fair I make Casper the ghost look dark.

'My step-sister Carmen always had this make-up set on her desk so I thought it would be a nice present to get you.'

Carmen looks like a beautiful Italian model, she and I have completely different faces and personalities. It is the thought that counts I guess, that's what I am going to keep telling myself anyway. Maybe it will be third time lucky?

I pull the remaining present out of the cardboard box. Again it is rectangular and the size of a coaster mat, which means it could literally be anything.

'I saw this and immediately thought it would be your style. I just had to get it for you.'

Now I am intrigued. It is clearly fashion related. It must be a brooch or maybe a small silk scarf or… I stop trying to second guess what it is and lift the lid on the box to reveal my gift.

What in the name of Dickens is this.

After the haircut and the scooter and now this I begin to wonder whether Laurence has been consuming mind altering drugs or is constantly drunk, as this gift is definitely not my style.

As if picking up a dirty sock, I lift one of the huge bright yellow and plastic pineapple earrings. I have never worn earrings like this in my life. I always wear a pair of studs in my ears, and if I am really going to town I will put in my gold hoops, not a fucking fruit basket.

'They are so cool aren't they!'

Yes, if you live on a tropical island and sell fruit smoothies, I want to say to him. Instead I just smile and place the earring back in the box and gently close the lid, hoping they will never see the light of day ever again. I try really hard to look pleased with the gift in order not to disappoint him and to convince myself not to be so ungrateful for the gifts he has given me.

'You are going to wear them tonight aren't you? They will look so good with your red dress.'

I immediately try and think of an excuse but Laurence is staring at me with his big blue puppy eyes. And so like the sucker I am, and the fact I can't seem to find the guts to tell him they are bloody awful I put them in my ears.

Forget Laurence being blind drunk, It looks like I am going to have to get plastered this evening just to forget I am wearing these hideous lumps of plastic in my lobes.

Laurence helps me put the discarded wrapping paper back in the cardboard box and my other presents beside it. To be honest I doubt I would be upset if Mum threw out both piles of stuff and thought it was rubbish, I might even be grateful for it. We then head into the kitchen to have a slice of birthday cake before we go out.

As I enter the kitchen, I see that Mum's eyes have become the size of saucers and Dad nearly spits out his tea into his mug as they eye the horrendous neon pineapples that are dangling from my ears.

'Did you buy Ruby those earrings Laurence? They are very unusual.', Mum says desperately trying to pretend everything is normal.

'They're pretty groovy aren't they Mrs Samuels.'

Who an earth in this day and age says something looks 'groovy'. Forget him being drunk, I think he has been abducted by aliens.

'Well yes, I suppose that is one way of describing those earrings.'

I can see that Mum is trying to subtly suggest to Laurence that maybe these earrings don't suit me. On the other hand Dad is trying not to snort anymore tea up his nose.

'I think Ruby looks lovely in them,' which Laurence then follows up with a peck on my cheek.

I try to pretend, for Laurence's sake, that I really do like these earrings, despite the fact I look like Pat Butcher from *EastEnders* in them.

As we make our exit and I close the kitchen door behind us, I can hear Dad howling with laughter and say; 'Well Mop A Top certainly gave Ruby a gift to remember this year for her birthday.'

Thankfully Laurence was too busy on his phone, working out the best way to get to the pub from the house to hear what was said. I am not sure why Laurence is asking the internet for directions as all we have to do is walk up the road to the tube station and get off at the next stop, the pub is right opposite the station.

Rather than questioning him, I leave him be as I want my birthday night to go as smoothly as possible, plus I need time to think of how to 'accidentally' lose these earrings tonight.

After telling me it will take us exactly twenty minutes to get to our destination if we walk at a brisk pace, Laurence and I make our way out of my parent's hallway, where I leave my coat on the rack, and step into the still warm June night. I take a moment to enjoy the balmy air on my skin and then feel Laurence wrap his arms around my waist bringing me closer to him. I fall into his embrace and feel his freshly shaven face up against my cheek as he plants a kiss on it;

'I love you Ruby. You have made me such a happy man.'

In response I smile and give him a kiss on the lips, my stomach full of butterflies and my face feeling rosy. I too feel so happy right now, so much so I don't even care about those sodding earrings dangling in my ears anymore but despite these feelings I still don't feel ready to utter those same three words back to him. I want to say them but I just can't.

Luckily Laurence doesn't seem to notice my lack of response and we instead walk hand in hand towards the pub.

CHAPTER 18

'Nothing compares… Nothing compares to yoooooouuuuu…'
There is nothing like a bit of Sinead O'Connor to really make
you feel shit about your love life as you lie in bed on a Saturday
morning. I whack the volume up to full and let the music deafen
my eardrums in the hope it will stop me moping about Ruby and
how she is still out of my grasp. In fact it's been more than seven
hours and fifteen days since I last heard from her. Listening to
Ms. O'Connor is probably not the best song to help me move
on. Ever since I arrived in England, my music tastes have
become more and more morose, at this rate I am going to be
listening to white noise to get me through the day.

Although my love life has gone down the toilet, my work life is
doing much better as 'Knobhead Neil' has been told to pack his
bags and go home. When he was packing his stuff, several
members of the office began to clap and shout out 'good
riddance' so I doubt he will be sorely missed here. Harsh, but
what comes around goes around.

He left due to an 'incident' that took place two weeks ago. For
some reason 'Knobhead Neil' had difficulty controlling his urges
at work when it came to Karen, so decided it would be a good
idea to give her a good seeing to in the stationery cupboard at
work. Karen, unfortunately has an inability not only to keep her
legs shut but her mouth too and told anybody who looked like

they were listening, about her and Neil's 'naughty antics' in the cupboard. This information, regrettably for Neil, got passed to the Chief Executive of Charter and Charter who was making a special visit to the London office from Sydney. Due to his previous unprofessional behaviour in Australia and the fact he hasn't met any of his targets this year, his time was up or as the Terminator likes to say; *'Hasta la vista, baby.'*

Neil and Karen also forget that due to the high price biros and post-it notes are reaching these days there is a security camera in the cupboard, so despite Neil and Karen claiming nothing serious happened and it was just office gossip, the CCTV tape proved otherwise.

I feel sorry for the poor bastard who had to watch the carnal mess that those two created in that cupboard. I've even become paranoid as to whether any of my stationary is clean to use or whether it ended on top, behind or somewhere else unpleasant between them. I've been making heavy use of the Dettol wipes that Natalie keeps on her desk. Natalie is the receptionist that has replaced Karen, she's a pretty cool chick actually. If I wasn't so hung up on Ruby I would probably ask her out on a date. I could take her to *WH Smith* as clearly stationery gets people going in this office.

It also doesn't help that Uncle Terry still has the 'no girls' rule at the flat even after Madonna-gate a few months ago. Luckily everyone is now all cool about it and since I caught Uncle Terry in his full drag persona of Theresa, and the fact that Chad and I couldn't give a flying fandango what he likes to dress up as, he has really embraced the more feminine side of himself. When myself or Chad have come home from work we have found sequins in the most peculiar of places, make up in the bathroom and false eyelashes and bottles of tanning lotion in the bin. Despite having to check twice that there isn't any glitter on my shirt collar before I go to work I am happy that Uncle Terry finally feels comfortable to show us who he really is and can now

152

understand why Mum thinks he is a barrel of laughs.

Terry's Teriyaki Tuesday has also become a regular occurrence and often occurs on other days of the week, the curfew rule he had in place has now gone and is now replaced with Chad and I trying to out-do Terry and his attempts at signing Bon Jovi at the local karaoke bar. I am still working on the no-girls rule, I think he feels that the girls we might bring back will judge him, that or he thinks they might steal his clothes, whatever it is I need to change his thoughts on it.

Personally I think he needs to forget the tassels and diamantes and spend his spare time setting up a food truck, as the food he cooks is out of this world. I told him this and his response was;

'Do you really think the likes of me, a glamorous man in his forties look like I belong on a food truck dishing out burgers to spotty looking teenagers. A life on a truck is not for me darling.'

And with that he twirled around and headed back to his record player to put on some Shirley Bassey. I'm not sure who he is kidding, he certainly is not in his forties.

Other than enjoying time with Uncle Terry I haven't being going out and enjoying the rest of the city as I just don't have the interest or the energy especially after my stomach is beginning to swells to the size of a small football after eating all this rich food Uncle Terry cooks us.

I need to start making more of an effort to do things in my life though rather than eating and boozing. I might see if I can book a trip out of London and into the countryside, maybe head to somewhere like Suffolk. I have no idea what is there but I like the sound of the place.

As I sit up on my bed, I pull my laptop towards me and begin googling weekend getaways to Suffolk. Suddenly my phone begins to buzz across my bedside table.

It buzzes once, meaning it is a text message rather than a phone call and in my current lazy state I wonder if I can be bothered to reach over and see who it is. Most likely it is Chad giving me another update of his location in London. Not sure why he does that or why he is going out and about to all these places without me. I haven't spent much time with Chad recently where it is just the two of us. I should make this more of a priority and just check in with him to see if he is okay. I have offered to join him on his trips about town but every time he does he says he would rather go on his own. Rather unusual for Chad as he used to hate being on his own, maybe this is his way of coping with moving to a new country or maybe he is meeting someone else? Or maybe he is just embarrassed at the current state of his friend.

If it's not Chad who has messaged then it is probably Uncle Terry making sure I haven't stolen his lipstick or over watered his pot plants.

Despite trying to ignore it and continue enjoying the comforts of bed, my body automatically turns to the right and leans over with a groan and picks up the phone.

I take a sharp intake of breathe. It's Ruby.

> Hey Ryan. Sorry it's been a while. I am having a couple of drinks for my birthday tonight. Would be great to see you. Bring Chad as well if he is free. Let me know and I'll text you the details.
> X

Twenty minutes later I finally compose what I feel is a suitable text.

> Hey!! Happy Birthday! Text me the deets and I'll be there. X

After pressing send and getting the details back straight away, I feel a sudden burst of energy and fling the duvet away from me and start to think of what I could get Ruby for her birthday. I cannot believe I forgot today was her birthday, so much for being in love with her.

I look around my room to find some clothes and make the mistake of greeting myself in the bedroom mirror where I see a sad sack of a man. Pasty skin, two day old stubble and muscle turning to flab. Enough is enough. Time for an overhaul – new haircut, clothes and maybe a girdle to keep this stomach in…

Before I set off on my mission, I head to the shower, as it seems that eating last night's curry in bed wasn't as good of an idea as I thought, some of the chicken madras has made a home in the back of my hair.

* * *

Revitalised, clean and smelling of patchouli, I head to the shops. I presume the fragrant smell is patchouli as that's what it said on the side of Uncle Terry's shower gel bottle. Knowing my luck it will bring me out in hives as karma for 'permanently borrowing' his shower gel.

I'll get him a new one… eventually. Maybe some *Lynx Africa* stuff, I am sure that will send the boys around him wild.

I feel optimistic about the day ahead, the sun is shining, and I feel I am getting back to being the confident and suave gentleman I am.

As I get to the entrance of *Westfield* shopping centre I feel all my optimism drain away as there are hundreds of shops in here and I have no idea where to go.

I decide to text Chad. I need to tell him about tonight anyway. I am hoping he is free and not off on one of his secret trips again. He is good at buying girls gifts, he'll know what to do.

Yo Dude! Ruby is having b-day drinks tonight. She's invited us both. You free to come?

Sweet. I'm in. It's at The George isn't it?

How does he know the location? I haven't told him and Ruby said to invite Chad so I presumed she hadn't contacted him. Unless they have been talking more than I know? I'm starting to worry I'm losing my best friend as well as my hopes of a love life. On that topic I better text back;

Yep it's The George. What do you think I should get her for a present?

I dunno. A bunch of flowers or something?

What a great gift to get a florist; flowers. Jeez. Thanks a bunch Chad. I think about phoning Mum to see if she could come up with some better ideas but it is the middle of the night back home and even if I did ring, I would probably end up speaking to that pathetic boyfriend of hers. My skin is crawling just at the thought of it.

Think Ryan. Think. I begin pacing up and down the shop windows to see if it will spark any ideas. I go past a toy shop, maybe she likes *Lego* or maybe a teddy bear. No that's no good, she will be 28 not 12. Those are gifts a guy gives to his daughter not a girl he wants to be with. Okay next shop… *Ann Summers*, it appears to be a lingerie shop. Lingerie would be a pretty brave choice of present and would probably result in a slap from her or her boyfriend, and I'd be gutted that he could end up taking the lingerie off rather than me, besides I don't know Ruby's size yet. Despite knowing this isn't a sensible gift choice for her, I have a closer look at what's in the shop window. It's been a while since I got some action.

Woah Ann is quite a dirty girl, PVC and crotchless knickers seem to be the main outfit choices for these mannequins. The stuff in the shop window is pretty saucy, just goes to show these buttoned-up Brits like to let loose and button-down in the bedroom.

Don't get distracted Ryan, you only have a few hours until the party and you still need to get a haircut and find some clothes to wear. Plus Ruby still has a boyfriend so I need to reel myself in a bit and remind myself of the boundaries.

Just as I get out of my daydream, I hear a woman shout at me. She looks as though she has walked straight off the set of Jeremy Kyle with her grubby face and grey tracksuit and unfortunately thinks that I am ogling her rather than daydreaming about Ruby.

'Oi, what are you looking at you pervert?'

I feel as if the whole shopping centre has stopped to stare at us. If I was a brave man I would respond with; 'You, you big fat whale and why Greenpeace haven't pushed you back in the water yet.'

Instead I remain silent and hope this troll goes back to her cave. Thankfully all she does is grunts and stuffs the iced doughnut she is holding right into her big gaping mouth. It doesn't even touch the sides.

The store next to *Ann Summers* is a card shop, so I dive in there and hope that Tubby McTub face has choked to death on her doughnut or has found some other man she can harass and get her kick for the day.

Right, back to the task at hand. I just want a nice plain card with the words; 'Happy Birthday' written on it. This should be simple enough. I look at the shelves in front of me and they seem to go on forever and ever. There's big cards, small cards, cards that play a tune, cards that are 3D, cards that wish Happy Birthday to a friend, not quite a friend, maybe a friend, and almost like a dad friend. Argggghhhhh… there is just too much choice. I feel myself getting hot and bothered and wonder whether all this effort for Ruby is really worth it.

It is so much easier to buy a gift for a guy. All you need to do is buy them a pack of beer and you're sorted. No need for a card. The only people who ever want a card are women. Women want a card for everything, they would even send a card to say thank you for a thank you card. Madness.

I eventually calm down and decide to grab one from the humorous section which isn't too crude or too corny. I double check the card to make sure it doesn't say 'Happy Birthday Aunt' or something else which could make things awkward. The card has a monkey on the front, laughing and holding a banana. If I were him I'd be laughing too about how much of a mug I am getting worked up about a bloody card.

I quickly pay for the card before I go bananas with the stress of it all, one card down, one present to go. Maybe I should just get her a gift voucher for somewhere; a boring but safe option. I cautiously exit the shop in the hope Tubby McTub face has left the vicinity, the coast is clear and I begin my journey around the rest of the shopping centre hoping I can now find a suitable gift.

Suddenly my eye is caught by the most beautifully decorated shop front, 'Leonardo's' is written in gold italic writing at the top and the window is decorated as if it was an enchanted forest with wooden owls, felt foxes and green paper leaves highlighting the shops product. In the left hand corner I see the star of the show. This gift is perfect for Ruby.

CHAPTER 19

The journey to the pub seemed to go on forever and ever. I felt so awful not being able to say the words 'I love you' back to Laurence. The words whir around my head but every-time I try to face Laurence to say them my body freezes, incapable of providing the words he deserves to hear back.

When we eventually arrive at the pub I push open the large oak doors, and are greeted with the traditional woody and alcohol soaked smell every old English pub has, it feels comfortable and warm, although probably a little too warm for a balmy summer evening as tonight. I take a moment to look around the vast sized pub and see Catrina, along with her flatmates sitting in one corner on a green leather bench next to a round mahogany table and Laurence's friends sitting in the other corner on a similar looking bench.

Laurence's friends are all sitting hunched over the table and each are taking turns to slowly sip their pint as they discuss the intricacies of whether Batman is better than Superman.

I look back over in Catrina's direction, she is smiling and looking lovely in a red floral tea dress, which highlights the natural red blush of her cheeks. Catrina is just one of those girls who has such warmth to her that if you saw her at a bus stop you would naturally just want to strike up a conversation with her. Yet the three girls she is sitting with, look like they had been sucking lemons for the past hour. If it wasn't for their different hair colour, you would struggle to tell them apart.

I hear one of the clones loudly whisper to the others; 'So this is the birthday girl, is it?'

She slowly eyes me up and down and the other two join in with their disapproving looks of me.

'Catrina go and get me a drink as I am parched. I think it's your round anyway.'

'It was my round last time. It's your turn now Terri-Ann' says Catrina firmly.

They all ignore her and Terri-Ann says in response;

'I'll have a gin and tonic please.'

Catrina rolls her eyes and crosses her arms. She is clearly determined to stand her ground, and good for her, it's about time she tells those girls where to go. They are clearly not her friends, they just use her for a source of entertainment and to help pay the rent. I just hope she can find herself somewhere else to live soon, putting up with those witches must be unbearable.

One of Laurence's friends comes striding towards us and prevents me from getting any closer to Catrina. I recognise him from a few socials I've been to before with Laurence. His name is Eddie and he has that stereotypical geek look, in fact he could be a double for *McLovin*. He has arrived with John, Steve and Dan. All of them wearing the staple uniform of the cagoule (always in grey, navy and black and always zipped up to the top), blue jeans, glasses, a rucksack and hiking boots, the ultimate survival gear for a night out in Essex. Eddie completely ignores me and heads straight for Laurence instead, clearly intent to tell him what's on his mind.

'You're late. You said you would be here at 7pm. It is now 7:15pm. You should have changed the invite to 7:15pm if you knew you weren't going to be here until then.'

Now when someone invites you to drinks or to a party and they say to come round at 7pm, generally that means you come round some time after 7pm. Of all the parties I had been to and been invited to before I met Laurence you turn up around 8pm at the earliest if the invite says 7pm. However, when your boyfriend has friends who are highly particular, you have to be specifically clear what time you expect them otherwise it messes with their daily schedule and for everyone's sake you do not want to mess with their schedule. Seeing a grown man hysterically crying knowing they have missed the next episode of *Game of Thrones* because we were late is not a pretty sight.

Despite his rant, he does manage to find some manners and wishes me a 'Happy Birthday', although the way he said it would make C-3PO seem more human.

I smile back at him and thank him for his birthday wishes. He then looks straight back at me, appears to open his mouth to say something else but instead he goes bright red in the face, and retreats to the safety of his cagoule gang. He has probably gone into shock after talking to a female this evening that wasn't his mother.

Finally I make my way over to Catrina as originally planned. She is so pleased to see me, her flatmates less so as they physically turn their backs to me. I see Catrina cringe at their behaviour, so I do my best to keep everything upbeat and positive.

'Hey! How are you? You look lovely this evening.'

'Happy Birthday Ruby!' She responds loudly and cheerfully.

We both give each other a strong bear hug, which almost rips these horrendous pineapple earrings out of my ear.

I've bought you a little something. It's from me and Andre. I hope you like it. He was gutted he couldn't be here but says he will buy a chocolate cake and eat it in your honour. Bit rude if you ask me.'

Typical Andre, one day I will have to tell Catrina about the chocolate cake incident.

She gently pulls my left hand closer to her and then using her other hand delves into her handbag and pulls out a thin blue beaded bracelet with a small gold rose charm on it. She nestles it neatly in the palm of my hand.

'The rose is made from Welsh gold. So whenever you wear it, there will always be a little bit of Wales with you and a reminder to you of me and Andre.'

I immediately want to cry. The bracelet is incredibly beautiful, it is so delicate and intricately crafted. I am lost for words and hope a big long hug will convey my thoughts of deep gratitude for this gift. This is the most wonderful gift anyone has ever given me. Andre and Catrina are friends that are beyond amazing. I just wish I had been more of a friend to Catrina these past weeks than she has been to me.

I put the bracelet on immediately. Both of us look like we are on the verge of crying tears of joy.

I give Catrina another hug to further cement my gratitude and as I do so, I hear a familiar voice behind me.

'I didn't realise your birthday drinks was 80s themed – Chad and

I could've dressed as Wham! for the occasion.'

I turn around to face him and he gives me a wink and I feel my knees begin to tremble. After everything I have been through, why oh why does he have this effect on me?

As I take a split second to look into his captivating green eyes, I feel a hand on my arm and turn to see that it is Laurence.

Unfortunately Laurence doesn't take too kindly to Ryan's joke.

'It's not a themed night. Although if it was I am sure you guys would win top prize as the Chuckle Brothers.'

Ouch. Luckily Ryan being Australian probably has no idea who the Chuckle Brothers were and if he did, he didn't show it, he just smiled a smile that made Laurence look inferior.

Laurence releases my arm and turns away to greet some more of his work friends who have just arrived and thankfully are more human-like than Eddie and his gang. During all this commotion Catrina and Chad have disappeared and I am left standing all alone with Ryan.

There is an awkward silence, and I need to fill it before something stupid happens. He looks so handsome tonight.

'Don't get me started about these bloody things.' I say swinging the plastic earrings back and forth in my ears.

'They were a gift from Laurence. If I could bin them I would. I feel like I should be breaking out a rendition of 'Agadoo.''

Ryan lets out a small smile, making him look even more gorgeous. I am so close to him right now I can smell his aftershave and am almost in kissing distance of his beautiful smooth lips.

He gently pushes back my curly hair and my heart feels like it is about to pound out of my chest. What is he doing? He leans in closer and I begin to wonder whether I should back away. He can't kiss me in front of all these people even if I wanted him to. To my relief he avoids my lips and whispers something in my ear.

'I have something for you Ruby.'

I feel the tension rise in me again and I do my best to make the situation as light as possible.

'Please don't tell me it's a fruit basket or I might just have to pour that pint you ordered all over your head.'

He laughs out loud, a throaty and sexy laugh. A laugh that is dangerous and is making me want him too much.

He leans down and reaches into the plain tote bag on the floor, as I make myself comfortable on the nearest bar stool. He pulls out a rectangular package wrapped in brown paper and parcel string, on top is a purple envelope. My adrenalin is so high, I swear my vision is starting to go blurry, although this might be down to the fact Mum and Dad got me to drink some celebratory Pina Colada's earlier today and the effects are starting to kick in.

'Open the card first,' he says gently, placing a hand on my knee, which he quickly takes away again.

I say nothing, as my slowly reddening face does the talking for me. I take my time gently tearing open the envelope, avoiding all eye contact with Ryan.

I then slip the card out of the envelope to reveal a picture of a monkey holding a banana saying; 'It's your day to go bananas.'

'I told you what I would do if I saw anything fruit themed.'

He takes a swig of the pint the barmaid has just handed him and gives me a cheeky grin;

'Hopefully the writing inside will be more to your taste.'

I open the card up and see he has written me a message in blue ink and in the most neatest of handwriting. The message reads:

'Dear Ruby, Another year older, although maybe not another year wiser. ;-) Continue to be bold, beautiful and chase your dreams. Love Ryan x'

Well that really has got me in the feels. This guy is good, he knows the exact buttons to press. I decide to take his advice of being bold and look him straight in the eye, thank him, and return his brief touch of my knee to him.

He does nothing to prevent my touch, in fact if it wasn't for a flicker in his eyes, you would have thought it would have caused him no feelings what so ever. Just friends, I remind myself, that is all this can ever be.

'Now open your present. I am really excited for you to see this. And please be quicker than your card opening, I don't want to still be sitting here for your next birthday waiting for you to unwrap it.'

I take this as a challenge and take an agonising amount of time undoing the parcel string. I look up at him and he rolls his eyes and taps his watch so I tear right into the paper, my heart hammering as I do so. As I brush the paper on to the floor, I take a moment to look at the gift. It is a smooth wooden box with two silver metal clasps on the front. After today's gifts, I decide to keep my expectations of the contents low.

'Is this going to be one of those trick presents where all I am going to be doing is opening different boxes to reveal nothing at the end?'

'Open the box and you'll find out.'

As I open the wooden box I am confronted with a world of colours. It really is magnificent. Inside are a rainbow of paints and neatly displayed brushes and inside my heart begins to sing.

I have often looked at sets like this in artist supply shop windows or online and always wished for one, exactly like the one in front of me, it was just time and money that had prevented me in doing so.

Since opening the shop I haven't drawn or painted a single thing as I always seem to find an excuse not to sit down and sketch something. My one true passion and I have neglected it. Ryan's gift is just what I need right now, to remind me of what I really love and what I yearn to be; an illustrator. A very good present from a very good friend.

'Wow… Ryan I am absolutely speechless. This is perfect, thank you so very much.' I give him a quick peck on the cheek to show my appreciation and his face begins to redden as much as mine has, both unsure how to deal with being 'just friends'.

'Well a special girl deserves a special gift. Besides I haven't seen you post any of your artwork online recently but now you have some new paints you have no excuse not to get back into it.'

He is pushing my heart too far, I need Laurence to come back and control our behaviour. In fact, where is Laurence? I scan the busy pub to see if I can locate him and see that he appears to be engrossed in discussing the merits of something boring with the cagoule gang, allowing temptation to take a step closer.

'It's getting a bit hot in here, how about we go outside for a bit to get some air.'

To be honest my face is now the same colour as my dress, so there is a bit of truth to it but also I have a craving to be able to talk freely with Ryan without anyone else looking and listening.

He finishes the remnants of his pint and nods. As I collect the paper from the floor and put it back in the tote bag with my gift, I do a quick scan of the pub to see if anyone will notice us going outside. Surprisingly, everyone else seems to be engaged in conversation in their own little groups, so much for coming out and celebrating my birthday.

Like a true gentleman Ryan opens the door for me and we quietly slip out into the cool night. He is right behind me, his solid body touching my back. I quickly move forward to avoid any lingering contact and to ensure I do nothing to compromise my relationship with Laurence. Kind, caring and loyal Laurence. I shouldn't be doing anything stupid to ruin our relationship yet here I am outside on my own with Ryan.

Across the pub car park I see Chad and Catrina. Why are they out here together? Is this who Catrina had been texting recently? I really should have been more attentive to her as a friend as she has been to me. By the looks of their faces they are in engaged in quite a tense and serious conversation.

I look at Ryan and he looks as shocked as I do that Catrina and Chad are out here together. He gently grabs my arm and we head round the side of the pub so they don't spot us but where we can still secretly watch them from afar. Ryan positions himself behind me again and whispers;

'Chad kept banging on about Wales the other day. I just thought he wanted to be a sheep farmer. I didn't figure it was to do with your mate Kate.'

'Her name is Catrina you idiot. She even wears a name badge in the shop which clearly states her name is Catrina. Shows how much you pay attention.'

I roll my eyes at him and in return he shrugs his shoulders.

'If your such a mate to Kate… Catrina… whatever her name is how did you not know what was going on with her and Chad?'

Before I can respond and feel any further guilt at being such a shit friend there is suddenly a loud burst of noise;

'ARE YOU ASHAMED OF ME? IS THAT IT? IS THAT WHY YOU WON'T TELL PEOPLE WE ARE TOGETHER OR MAYBE ALL I WAS TO YOU WAS A ONE NIGHT STAND. A ONE NIGHT STAND WITH A CHUBBY WELSH GIRL.'

Catrina is so loud, she makes a megaphone sound quiet.

Chad makes shushing noises in order to prevent anyone within a ten mile radius lodging a noise complaint but this just makes the situation worse.

'DON'T TRY AND SHUSH ME.'

Catrina then bursts into a flood of tears. I so desperately want to go over and comfort her and tell her everything will be alright but I know if I do she will discover I have been spying on her and after that beautiful moment of friendship we had in the pub earlier, I really do not want to jeopardise our relationship, even more so than the one I have with Laurence.

I see Chad trying to go over and comfort her but she is having none of it. Instead she tells him to 'stay away' and fishes a big tissue out of her bag and blows her nose which causes such a noise, you would've thought a ship had come into port. I do my best to stifle a laugh and I think I may have even see a slight curl of the lips from Chad too, even Ryan makes a quiet coughing noise behind me.

'Poor Chad. As his best friend I can tell you he really does love your friend Kat... er... um Catrina. He has that look about him. He is just not that good with words.'

'Poor Chad... more like poor Catrina, look at her she is crying her eyes out.'

'Sometimes with love things can get confusing.'

His right love is confusing. Our hands touch and he tries to weave his fingers through mine. I can feel my blood pumping in my ears and my shoulders begin to tense.

I want us to be entwined together, hand to hand, lip to lip, body to body but too much has happened between us and I am in a different place to where I was when I first had my brush of love or lust or whatever it was with Ryan. And I must remember Laurence.

I continue staring straight ahead at Chad and Catrina as if Ryan isn't here. They both seem to have calmed down a little although are making their way back to the pub separately, Chad skulking at the front and Catrina several steps behind desperately trying to regain her normal composure and clean up her mascara stained face.

'Sometimes in love you just have to let go,' I say with a sinking heart.

The words echo around the pub car park and I feel them punch me right back in the stomach. I turn to see Ryan's green eyes fill with disappointment and slowly begin to push his hand away from mine. I wish things weren't like this but Laurence has been the one who has been there for me and helped me with the shop and so honestly told me that he loves me. I have to be loyal to Laurence.

We decide to both head back in as we need to make sure our friends are okay, plus I have left my paint box inside, I need to make sure some moron hasn't painted his face with them, spilt beer on them or even worse stolen them. I intend to paint my best pictures with those paints.

CHAPTER 20

I keep thinking about that night. The night of Ruby's birthday. Despite the horrific earrings she was wearing, she still looked absolutely stunning, just like that first night when I saw her in Sydney. To quote the legend that is Cher, 'if I could turn back time…' I would.

When I gave her that gift, her beautiful blue eyes shone with pure delight. I keep desperately trying to move on but I just can't do it. She's settled with Laurence now and although he has a shit haircut and bad taste in presents for women he seems a decent guy and is utterly besotted with Ruby, she deserves someone decent like him who will look after her.

'Sometimes in love you have to let go.' Those words enter my head daily and the brief feel of her hand from that night still feels as raw and electric on my skin as it did a month ago. If only I had done something differently that night to convince her to change her mind about me.

Although I was luckless in love the night of Ruby's birthday, Chad on the other hand seemed to have Cupid well and truly on his side. After his argument with Catrina outside the pub, Ruby and I discreetly followed them a few seconds later. I was rather impressed by my stealthy moves, it made me think whether in a previous life I was a ninja or even a spy. I mean it is still not too late for me to join the secret services, I could make an excellent James Bond.

Secret Services aside, I needed to sort out Chad who had now positioned himself at the corner of the bar. I casually strolled over, see told you I could make an excellent spy, and then asked him whether he was okay.

He just point blank ignored me, crossed his arms, exhaled through his nose loudly and asked the barman for another pint. Shit me, he was angry. In the whole time I have known Chad, I have never seen him get this worked up about something.

I looked over to Catrina who also seemed to have flashes of anger burning across her face as it was bright red and carried a rather big frown. Although this could be because she was struggling to squash herself between two of Laurence's nerdy friends who were not too happy about being interrupted in the middle of another philosophical debate.

Chad saw what she was doing and looked away muttering to himself. Now when a guy is in this type of mood, it is often best to let him stew for a while and give him a moment to compose himself and process what is happening. The last thing they need is some annoying girl to start pestering them.

Yet one of Catrina's so called 'mates' decided to do just that. Having been around the block a bit, I know exactly what these girls are like. Too thin, too desperate and too up their own arse. This girl had tried to flirt with me earlier but I gave her the cold shoulder, knowing that she isn't worth the trouble even if I was looking to get laid.

As she launched her attack on Chad, she made sure to stand in front of me deliberately wiggling her bony arse in my direction at an attempt to show me what I'm missing. This girl is pathetic and desperate, and to think that I used to love girls like this.

'Excuse me...' she squeaked to Chad as she jabbed one of her acrylic pink nails into his shoulder.

Chad continued to stare deeply into his pint, pretending to be completely oblivious to this thin brunette, with her pumped up chest and spider eyelashes that she is desperately batting to get his interest.

Not one to give up, probably due to the fact she was slightly intoxicated from the alcopops she had been downing since she got here, she tried her luck with Chad again.

'EXCUSE ME!' Her voice was so loud everyone in the bar turned around to see what was happening. I quickly glanced over at Catrina and saw that she too was staring at Chad and this tart.

Chad finally decided to look at this girl, although he didn't have much choice after squawking at him like some deranged parakeet. Now she had his attention she flicked her hair to the side as if she was trying to recreate a scene out of Baywatch, which resulted in me having to quickly move my pint closer to my chest to avoid her hair taking a bath in it.

'G'day, can I help you Missy?' Chad said drily as he re-diverts his eyes back to his pint glass.

'Oooh I love your accent. Where are you from?'

He took another sip from his beer and responded; 'I'm from Kangaroo Land, mate.'

'Kangaroo Land, I've never heard of that place but it sounds exotic.' She twirled her hair around her fingers and began to pout in an ill-judged attempt to look 'sexier', instead she looked like she belonged in a fishmonger's shop.

I saw Chad try and stifle a smile and I drank some of my pint in order to stop myself from bursting out loud laughing.

She leaned in closer. Chad doesn't flinch. Most women who aren't as desperate as this girl would have just backed away as it was clear he wasn't interested. He had made no signals that would suggest he was out on the pull, she should've just given up there and then.

'Seeing as you are from a place where they like to hop, how about you come and hop over to my place tonight?'

She followed up her invitation up with a wink as if this would seal the deal between her and Chad.

I saw Chad redden round his neck a little and begin to play with his shirt collar.

'Well doll, I'm rather flattered you think I am worth rooting this evening but I am just not interested.'

He handles the situation like a true gentlemen. Again, most women would have accepted that answer and wished him a 'good night' but as expected with a 'Miss Up-her-own arse' she struggled to understand why Chad would reject her.

'You're single aren't you? I don't see any wedding ring on your finger. What's the matter with you?' The volume of her voice by the end of her last sentence had reached decibel proportions.

I could feel the whole pub looking in our direction, waiting to see if this situation was going to get more dramatic than the latest episode of *Neighbours*. Luckily Chad is a pretty chill guy 99% of the time so I hoped his chilled ways would get this woman to calm the fuck down.

'No, I am actually interested in someone else in this pub.'

'You what?! How can you be interested in someone else in this pub. I wipe the floor with these other girls here.'

This girl really needed to wind her neck in and invest in some glasses as there were several people in this pub who were better looking than her, in fact some of the men in this pub were better looking than her.

'COME ON TELL ME WHO THIS GIRL IS THEN.'

Chad remained unfazed, he was no longer looking at this girl but instead was staring straight across at Catrina. Catrina was staring back at him, both of them wide eyed and unsure how to act on their emotions.

The girl or 'Megaphone Megan' as I will now affectionally refer to her had after a few drunken seconds clocked on to who Chad was looking at.

'You mean her?' she said as she jabbed her pointy acrylic tipped finger in Catrina's direction.

Chad nodded his head and smiled shyly at Catrina.

'How can you like her, she's fat, ugly AND Welsh.'

I looked over at Catrina and saw her bottom lip begin to tremble. Other than Ruby who was being restrained by Laurence, no one moved an inch from where they were, mesmerised by the drama that was unfolding in front of them.

Chad meanwhile sunk the rest of his pint, got up, looked Megaphone Megan square in the eyes and said to her calmly and clearly;

'You are mistaken. She is a beautiful Welsh woman and one you will never compare with.'

Megaphone Megan is left dumbstruck, unable to think of a clever enough comeback from the dressing down she has just received from Chad. She looks to her clique for support but none of them will give her eye contact, embarrassed to even be associated with her.

Chad then walked past Megaphone Megan and towards Catrina, who was now curled up like a hedgehog ready for hibernation. Chad lent in close to Catrina, lifted her chin and gave her direct eye contact.

'I'm sorry for being a dickhead. Forgive me?'

Before Catrina even had a chance to reply, he kissed her fully on the lips, to which the whole pub erupted in cheers and wolf whistles.

Megaphone Megan on the other hand scowled, barked at the other mean girls to exit and left muttering to herself that these people don't realise how lucky they were to have her in their presence.

After a passionate embrace, Catrina confirmed to Chad that she does forgive him but only on the condition that 'he kisses her like that everyday'. At that point the bartender shouted out;

'A free drink to the happy couple!'

I caught Ruby's eye for what would be the final time that night and we both shared a smile, knowing that we have witnessed something special; true love.

After everything that happened last night and despite my current desire to get Ruby back, it is time to listen to what the Universe is telling me. She is not the one. That's why I have decided to get myself back out on the dating scene and have asked our new receptionist Natalie to come round for dinner, she is the

176

complete opposite of Karen our previous receptionist, thank the lord, she is very quiet and unassuming in fact she rather reminds of the singer Natalie Imbruglia but with an English accent, although I hope she doesn't bring round a guitar and sing to me that would be awkward on so many levels. It will be nice to finally have a girl round to Uncle Terry's pad. Unfortunately the rules about girls are still in place it is just that he is off on holiday to Benidorm for a few weeks with his 'friend' Barry. But what he doesn't know won't kill him.

Even though I am keeping expectations low with Natalie, I really am hoping I will get laid this evening as it has been quite a dry spell and there are only so many exercises you can do with your wrists.

The doorbell rings. I look at my watch, it's too early for Natalie, she's not due round for another hour. I bet you it's one of those bloody Jehovah Witness's. There used to be one or two floating about in Australia trying to convert people to a lifetime of boredom but since coming to London, it's like they are on a continuous conveyer belt, week after week they come knocking at the door, always with their kids as well, so you can never be rude and tell them to fuck off. With Chad still out, I prepare my best fake smile and prepare to politely decline my need to be saved but as I open the door I see that the universe has answered my previously neglected prayers…

CHAPTER 21

Receiving those paints from Ryan has reignited the flare of creativity within me. I feel such a thrill when I put one of the light and perfectly formed brushes in my hand. It felt so good when I pressed the bristles in the paint and then against the paper, the colours are so magnificent it makes my heart sing.

My first painting was of a bunch of bright yellow daffodils that were on display in the shop window and from that moment on my true love of art has reappeared. As soon as I have a spare moment in the shop a brush or a pencil is in my hand and I am off creating my own perfect world. It feels good to get back to the true me.

A few weeks ago I put some of the paintings I had done up behind their corresponding real-life flowers in order to decorate the displays and cover up some of the plain plastic holdings the flowers were sat in.

I was hoping Laurence would say something meaningful about them when he came to help me close up but all I got was 'their nice'. Not quite the vote of confidence I was expecting, I would've have preferred it if he told me they were crap rather than nice so I wouldn't have to worry about looking like a fool in front of the customers when they entered the shop the next day. I spent the whole night tossing and turning, not getting a wink of sleep fretting about it all but thankfully the customers seemed to like them, in fact one customer asked if they were for sale.

Maybe Laurence is being reserved about my paintings as I spend so much time in the shop and painting that I hardly spend any time with him. I need to make Laurence more of a priority in my life. I need to make sure I don't lose him especially as he hasn't been his usual self lately.

Take last week, when I went up to our flat to see how he was getting on at work and to hand him his 3 o'clock cup of tea, he immediately slammed down his laptop lid and said he was 'fine'. I don't know why he was so rattled as he knows every day at 3pm I always pop my head upstairs to see how he is and to discuss the latest web design project he was working on. At the time I put it down to him experiencing a stressful day at work but then another red flag in my head popped up a few nights later when he had to take a private phone call.

Laurence never does private phone calls. He wanted our relationship to be open and honest about everything, it is one of the foundation stones of our relationship and why we work so well together. On the night in question we were on the sofa, I in my pyjamas, Laurence in his joggers and sweatshirt, both curled up together watching yet another crime documentary, as you can see we have the most romantic taste in TV, when suddenly his phone rang. Normally he would've ignored the call or answered it in my presence whilst I pressed pause so we don't miss any of the gory details but this time he stormed straight out of the room not even looking in my direction and shut the door firmly behind him.

His knee-jerk reaction made me curious so I tip-toed to the door and pressed my ear against it, okay yes I was checking up on him but I'm sure most girlfriends would do the same when their boyfriend suddenly bolts out of the room. I really had to push my whole body against the door to hear any sort of sound and although most of it was muffled, I did hear the following;

'Thanks Hayley, that would mean a lot if you could do that.'

Do what? We generally rely on one another to help each other out. What could another woman be assisting him with? I'm pretty sure it wasn't a work colleague as he has never mentioned the name Hayley before. I am not the jealous type but why was he speaking to a girl in private. What is he hiding from me?

When the conversation appeared to have come to an end I quickly crept back to the sofa and as he came back in, I casually asked who it was, and in response he snapped; 'Don't be so bloody nosey.'

The response startled me, it is very unlike Laurence to behave like that. I've been keeping a close eye on him recently and it's putting a strain on our relationship. He claims that over the past two weeks I have been like his shadow as every time he turns I am there, which isn't quite true as I have been spending most of my time on the shop floor.

I can feel a big argument between us brewing and as much as I hate confrontation, maybe I do need to have it out with him to clear the air and to settle my fears that he isn't chatting up other girls. I feel sick at just the thought of it. I really hope there is an innocent explanation to this.

***

As I try to block out the thought of Laurence spending time with another girl by rearranging the already perfectly placed lilies by the till, he suddenly appears in the shop.

'Hello gorgeous', he says planting a gentle kiss on my forehead.

'All the Saturday deliveries are now done, although I just need to make one more trip on that beauty out there…'

When Laurence refers to 'that beauty' he is referring to his sodding scooter. I have never understood why men become so obsessed with anything that has a motor in it. Every spare moment he has, when he isn't making strange phone calls or working, is spent keeping his scooter in 'tip top' condition. It is just a scooter, it really does not need that much attention. Although, as I am constantly reminded by Laurence, it isn't just a scooter 'it's a Lambretta, the epitome of cool'. Yeah sure. Despite my shared lack of love for his scooter, it has come in useful for helping me out with deliveries as they make up a lot of my trade on a Saturday.

Although I do worry about him going around on it in the city as there have been lots of reports in the news recently of men threatening delivery riders for their scooters, some of these drivers are lucky to be alive after being stabbed or getting acid thrown in the face. I pray Laurence never has to experience anything like that. There is also the risk that he could crash. Even though he may be a sensible rider, it doesn't mean everyone on the road also follows the highway code correctly.

Still on high alert from a few days ago I respond back with a hint of desperation in my voice. 'Where are you going? I can come with you. The shop is pretty quiet at the moment… And then we can spend a cosy night in together. I'm thinking we could watch that French film *Amelie*.'

There is a long pause as Laurence pretends to find a leaf on one of the lemon trees of immense interest, as he rubs the leaves up and down with his thumb and forefinger.

'Laurence you are avoiding the question. Where are you going?'

'I'm just visiting a friend, no need to get huffy about it.'

181

All I asked was where he was going. Most girlfriends ask their boyfriends these type of questions – don't they? Okay so he doesn't want me with him, maybe he wants some guy time but still… I don't like watching stupid films where you need subtitles to work out what they are saying, I just sit there and watch them because I know he likes them. Relationships are about compromises and he needs to start compromising by telling me where he is going even if he doesn't want me there.

I stand there staring at him in disbelief at the way he is acting but he carries on in his own little world as if I am not even there.

'Ah these lilies will be perfect for Ha-'

He stops mid-way through her name, I know exactly who is going to see now, that bitch Hayley. He looks me dead in the eye, knowing he shouldn't have mentioned even part of her name. His face is bright red from embarrassment but yet he still grabs the bouquet of lilies from the stand and scarpers out of the front door.

'Yeah… I got to go. See ya Ruby…'

As the bell on the shop door tinkles after his exit, I desperately try to clamber over the till counter to get to him before he goes off on his scooter. As I climb over in a fashion that Patsy and Edie from *Absolutely Fabulous* would be proud of, both denting my pride and my knee, I try to shout in his direction in the hope he will stop for a brief second and I can confront him once and for all.

'Are you going to pay for those flowers Laurence or is that slut Hayley going to cough up.' I shout, blood pouring down my knee and my dress somehow now caught in my knickers.

He can't hear me as his scooter engine is already purring and is seconds away from making his exit. I hobble to the door and slam it open. Despite my dramatic entrance on to the street he continues to turn his scooter around to head off. I shout for him to stop. He doesn't stop, instead he blows me a kiss, which I return with a look of disgust and he then rides off into the distance. I then see that in his rush to head off, a white piece of paper had fallen out of his jacket and is now flitting about in the small breeze.

It's probably a piece of rubbish but curiosity gets the best of me, so I chase after it, un-wedging my knickers from my dress en-route. As I pick up the piece I notice that it is an advertisement for a local business in a town just a few miles away. It's a jewellery business called 'Gemz' owned by a woman called 'Hayley Betteridge.'

Gotcha.

It's time to get to the bottom of this and find out the truth. But first, I need to sort out my knee before I leave a trail of blood in my wake.

***

After rummaging through the shop's first aid kit and resigning myself to the fact that my only plaster choice is one with Minnie Mouse on it, I need to have a word with Catrina about this, I head towards the train station to catch Laurence and Hayley red-handed.

When I finally arrive at the train station sweating and panting like a wild dog, fate appears to be on my side as there is a train at the platform and I jump straight on it. As the train trundles along to my intended destination, my non-injured knee is going up and down violently as I sit in anticipation, hoping I will be able to find 'Gemz' and get a view of Laurence and that woman, and find up what they are really up to.

'You have reached your destination.'

This is it. I increase my intake of breath as I step off the train to keep myself calm and hope it will decrease my sweating, from my armpits downwards it looks like two gerbils have pissed down my dress.

I try to walk briskly but calmly in order not to bring attention to myself from passers-by and in case I bump into someone I know. Essex is a much smaller place than people realise. As I turn the corner on to the main high street that's when I see it; the hideous eyesore that is 'Gemz'.

The shop looks small, although the garish pink neon sign above makes sure nobody misses it. Now I am here I am not sure what to do with myself and begin to wonder whether Laurence was actually heading here in the first place. He could be meeting Hayley elsewhere rather than at her shop or it could be a completely different Hayley entirely.

Then as if on cue Laurence turns up on his pale blue Lambretta with the lilies he snatched from my shop strapped to the back of his scooter. As he parks up outside the shop I decide to leap into action.

With my adrenalin now sky-high I begin to move like a ninja wearing clogs, I blame my bloody knee. I think about heading into a shop nearby to watch them undetected. I see a shop with potential that has the dreary and unimaginative name of 'Annabelle's', despite this I enter as it gives me a prime viewing position of Laurence and this mysterious woman he is visiting.

Immediately I am clocked by a thin woman who appears to be in her early thirties, her black hair scraped back into a tight bun and with an expression of someone who has just smelt dog turd. She is in head to toe black and has a pair of round specs which make her look like Edna Mode from *The Incredibles*.

184

She gives me the once over in my t-shirt dress and Minnie mouse plaster and immediately decides that I am not the type of clientele she would like to have in her shop.

'Are you looking for anything in particular?'

You can see she is trying to play it cool with me but I can see in her magnified eyes that she is squirming at the thought of me even touching the clothes in this shop.

'Just browsing,' I say confidently as I swoosh a hanger across one of the rails.

I see her flinch and her cool complex has suddenly disappeared as she says through tense teeth;

'Do not hesitate to call me over if you need help. No need to rummage through the rails, I can help you with anything you need.'

I politely smile and try to position myself in Annabelle's so I can get a good view of 'Gemz'. I go towards the shop window where a whole array of leather jackets are hanging and are labelled as 'weathered' but should be more accurately labelled as 'moth eaten', and stake my position.

I see that Laurence is now in the shop talking to what looks like a teenage boy who is clearly going through the 'emo' stage in his life as he is wearing all black and has a long black fringe to one side that he has to keep pushing back to keep out of his eyes. I think I can clearly rule him out as being Hayley.

Suddenly a woman appears by the counter. Fuck me. This woman is like Malibu Sindy on steroids. She has long peroxide blonde hair that sits just above her rather large bum yet despite the big booty she has the tiniest waist imaginable, lips like a trout and skin the shade of my parent's mahogany table, although I'm

185

not sure why she bothered doing herself up as a dogs dinner as it looks like she lets her chest do the talking.

What an earth could he see in her? Maybe he doesn't see anything in her, maybe I am just overreacting again and it's a cousin of his and he is just reconnecting with her or maybe Hayley has yet to appear. I suddenly feel someone else hovering around the same window I am looking at.

'There are some lovely items on that rack, all handmade. Please do let me know if they are of interest.'

Will this woman just fuck off. She knows damn well that I won't be buying anything. These jackets are £1,000 each and at that price I'd expect them to be lined with gold and not looking like the local tramp has handed it in. I have to be nice to this woman though as I need this viewing spot.

'I'm fine thank you,' I say tersely still keeping my eyes firmly fixed on 'Gemz'. It is then that I see Laurence hand over the lilies, lean over the counter to give her a hug followed by a kiss, which seemed to have been meant for the cheek but ends up being a brushing of lips. My heart stops. Although they parted quickly, Laurence made sure to look out the window to ensure no had seen him, how little does he know. I try to remain calm and not cry as I grip the clothes rail in front of me tightly.

'I am asking you to leave my shop, you have been here long enough now and have shown no interest in buying any of the items.'

With the anger and hurt boiling up inside of me I fling the jackets on to the floor and run out with tears streaming down my face.

She begins to shout out after me from the shop entrance as I continue running down the street. I look back at her with a look that would have made the girl from *The Exorcist* proud. I have no time to feel sorry for the way I acted or the consequences of my action as my head is too full of thoughts as to how to deal with what I have just witnessed. I eventually slow my run to a brisk walk as I catch my breath and curtail my anger. If he was unhappy why didn't he say anything? Why did he go into the arms of that bimbo rather than talk it out with me? Am I that difficult of a person?

I get back to a normal walking pace and head to the nearby park. Whenever I was stressed about exams or had a difficult problem to deal with I dealt with it by going for a long walk. It is my coping mechanism if I don't have any pens or pencils to hand. After the incident with Ryan in Australia, I paced the airport lounge so much, I wondered whether people thought I was acting 'suspiciously' but it did help to get my head straight and move forward with my life, well so I thought.

After a few laps around the park, avoiding people having picnics and young toddlers wandering aimlessly in the sunshine I morph back into a sensible and functioning adult that no longer wants to unleash Hulk-like smashes against clothing rails. The walking has helped bring a moment of clarity and decide what to do next. It's time to fix some things from the past.

As I exit the park and walk back through the high street to make my way to the tube station, I hear a horrendous noise as if two pieces of metal have scraped against each other. The direction of the noise is clearly behind me as I see people heading towards that way, with others clutching their hands across their mouths in horror and shock from what they have seen.

I don't want to look as I've dealt with enough carnage today. It is someone else's problem and I have too many of my own to sort out now.

CHAPTER 22

'Ruby whh…'

Before I even get a chance to finish my sentence she has pushed her lips straight on to mine. It feels good and I want to kiss her passionately back but first I want to know why she has suddenly had a change of heart and what the hell has happened to Laurence. The last thing I want to be is some girl's plaything. Ironic, considering not long ago I was vying for the position of Sydney's Playboy of the year.

It's interesting that there is the term of 'mistress' for males who have a woman as their bit on the side but not for men in the same position, although if they could give me a name in this situation it would probably be 'Mug'. I need to find out where I stand as I don't intend to be anyone's mug, spoon, fork or anything else until I know I am their number one priority and attention.

I push her firmly away from my lips and she gives me the sad doll look with her bright blue eyes that immediately make me want to put those lips back on to mine. She tries again to kiss me but I stay strong, keeping her at arms distance. There have been too many times where we have messed each other around in the pursuit of love for one another that I need to make sure we are both making the right decisions, although I am beginning to feel something stir in my trousers which is really not helping the situation, that dry spell has done me no favours at all.

'What about Laurence?'

Her face begins to pinken as if in embarrassment as to what has just happened and somewhat quickly she tells me how what I thought was my guilty pleasure of having Ruby's kiss just then, might not be so guilty after all;

'Okay I know this is out of the blue, and yes I am probably overreacting by kissing you like this but I want to make-up for lost time. After what I have seen today, Laurence is dead to me. I made a bad mistake leaving you when I got on that plane.'

She then explains what exactly has been going on between her and Laurence and I'm not really sure what to do or what to say. I hope she doesn't think that I am now her rebound whilst she gets over or gets back at Laurence. Yet there has always been a connection between us, I'm sure of it, although this could be what's down below talking right now rather than my head. I need to think clearly and keep my heart safe so it does not break again.

'I'm not your rebound Ruby. You know that I have feelings for you but I will not act on them when I know this is just a way for you to get back at Laurence. If you are looking for revenge then find a guy on GirlmeetsBoy to satisfy your needs. I want you forever not for a night.'

There is a fire in her eyes and her fingers are beginning to coil tightly round her ponytail in order to curb her frustration. This is not going to be easy.

Suddenly, her demeanour changes as she goes from swirling her ponytail around to holding her arms across her chest as if she is hugging herself, trying to give herself support.

'You're not a one night stand Ryan… you have and always will be more than that to me. In fact…'

She pauses and I see her lip begins to tremble.

Please don't cry Ruby, I say silently to myself, this is going to make this situation much worse than it already is for me.

'In fact…' she says squeezing herself tighter, '…I know this is going to sound silly and rather sudden but the truth is… I love you. I have never ever said this to anyone in my life, even Laurence. I've tried to stop myself thinking about you and trying to make it work with Laurence. It is only today, after what has happened that I've finally been truthful about my real feelings. We've wasted too much time and missed too many opportunities before. Let's not miss this one.'

I stand staring at her, dumbfounded. She loves me. She actually loves me. Those words I have been aching to hear from her for so long have arrived.

I look more intently at her and into those blue eyes and I see the honesty, I see the love and I see the passion she has for me; for us. I want to say the words 'I love you' back to her but something inside me is holding me back, almost as if this moment is too good to be true.

As I take a moment to figure out what to do next, my heart pumping with love, a strand of her pretty blonde curly hair escapes out of her ponytail, it gently frames her face and adds a softness to her pale clear skin.

I can't stand here any longer just staring at her and without the means of being able to verbally acknowledge her declaration of love, I will have to show her physically.

I push her against the wall and enjoy her soft full lips against mine. So what if this doesn't last and this does end up a one night stand? At least I would have got my kicks with someone I was lusting and then loving for after a long wait, and will hopefully make up for the rather long dry spell I imposed on myself. As she said, we've had too many missed opportunities to truly get together.

Before I have a chance to think further about my actions Ruby's hands have already made their way underneath my shirt and I am sure it won't be long until everything comes off.

Suddenly the doorbell goes. Fuck. Shit. Bollocks. That's probably Natalie trying to come in. I don't like hurting people's feelings as I have learned my lessons in the past not to be a douche when it comes to romance but I may need to break this rule in order to finally consummate my love with Ruby.

As I peel Ruby's hands away for me to deal with the unwelcome visitor, the door begins to swing open, revealing a face I have seen many times before.

'That fuckin' door needs to get sorted out. I'll have a word with ol' Tezza when he comes back from holiday and see if he has a moment in his sequin and glitter life to get it fixed.'

Thank God, it's just Chad with Catrina standing behind him. Both their eyes go wide in surprise to see me and Ruby here together with my shirt off and her dress slightly askew. Catrina then frowns at Ruby, confused as to what is going on.

'Does Laurence know about this?'

Part of me wanted to tell Catrina that he is on our way over to join in the fun just to see if I could make her eyebrows disappear off her forehead but I need Catrina and Chad to be on our side in case others disapprove of our relationship and besides this is something Ruby needs to deal with not me, I am the innocent party who has fallen for her charms not the other way round this time.

'Laurence isn't who he said he was,' she says defiantly whilst still clinging her arms tightly round my torso.

I feel like the cuddly toy grabbed in one of those claw machine you get at an arcade or fairground. Sweet that I have been chosen out of the other toys but also rather painful to be hanging in these claws until I am out of dangers way and connected with my new owner.

Catrina flabbergasted opens her mouth at an attempt but Chad quickly pulls up his hand in front of her mouth as a sign to close it, and loyally she does so.

'I'm sure these guys know what they are doing Catrina, no need to get yourself caught up in all. Although Ryan can you just answer me one question…'

What the hell does Chad want to ask me now, maybe he is trying to be the brain and think logically for me whilst I stand here pathetically encased in Ruby's strong grip.

'What's better Vegemite or Marmite?'

I laugh out loud, so much for asking me some deep and meaningful question about my relationship choices.

'Mate, that isn't even a question. It is quite clear that Vegemite is the best.'

'See I told you Catrina! Marmite is just shite. Admit it.'

'He would say that though, he is Australian. I think it is bloody disgusting. Whoever invented it needs to be shot. Besides if you live with me you'll have to get used to Marmite, I am not buying pots of sick to eat on toast when I can have the best spread in the world.'

'I'm sorry guys, but I am going to have to agree with Catrina, Marmite is much better than Vegemite. That's one of the things I missed living over in Australia,' says Ruby as she begins to loosen her grip around me.

'The two of you need to get your head checked. And Chad, looks like you'll need to buy your own jar of Vegemite when you live with Catrina.'

Chad laughs and in response Catrina sticks her tongue out. The conversation seems so comfortable between us all, as if we are already a pair of couples who know each other so well. This makes me even more sure that my decision to reunite with Ruby is the right one.

'Come on Catrina let's go and watch a film and maybe enjoy some of our own action later, show these two how to really get down.'

He gives a cheeky grin, winks at me and playfully slaps Catrina on the bottom as they make their way to the sofa. She lets out a small shriek and playfully hits Chad back and gives us a smile in return.

Charlie was an idiot to let him go but I know he and Catrina will be happy for many years to come. You know when you see couples and you just know they will be together forever, well Chad and Catrina look like one of those couples. I wonder if anyone would say the same when they would see me and Ruby together.

As Chad and Catrina settle onto the sofa in the lounge, I can be rest assured that it is now safe for Ruby and me to carry on our pursuit of carnal joy. I lead Ruby towards the bedroom ready to give her a night to remember. And then I remember Natalie.

Shit. She is probably due round any minute now. I tell Ruby to make herself comfortable in the bedroom and use the excuse of needing to go to the toilet so I can text Natalie in the hope she will piss off and won't be another woman I will need to add to the list of ruining my chances to sleep with Ruby.

I try to think of a good excuse to get rid of her as I pace up and down the tiny bathroom, each time I do I continually catch the eye of Uncle Terry's glittery bubble bath in the shape of a pig and I am hoping it gives me the answer out of this predicament.

```
Hi Natalie, it's me Ryan. I am going to have to
cancel tonight as I have swine flu.
```

```
              That sounds like an excuse to me. ;-) How long
                                    has this been going on?
```

It is Natalie, so maybe you should get the hint and leave me be so I can get my kicks with Ruby.

```
I am really going to have to cancel. I feel
absolutely awful, I've had it for a few days now
and have only had the energy to start texting
now.
```

I am going to rot in hell for the rest of time after this text but the lies are so worth the chance I have with Ruby right now.

```
        Well maybe a good back massage might help ease
                                    your recovery. ;-)
```

Jeez this girl is really persistent and its starting to make her look a little bit desperate now.

```
Nah I'm okay.
```

> Maybe I could get you some chicken soup or something to make you feel better?

> No, I will be fine.

> I'm sure I won't get infected if I just pop in and say a quick hello.

Christ almighty. She is really not getting the hint. I am going to have to be a bit firmer in my responses to her. Ruby is probably wondering what the hell I am doing in the bathroom for so long.

> Just don't come round.

> Okay dickhead. Nice knowing you.

Ouch that was harsh but probably well deserved. Besides there is no point dwelling on it as I have something much more exciting waiting for me in my bedroom. I can't wait to see her naked body.

I leave my phone in the bathroom to avoid my phone going off whilst in the bedroom, as I do not want any more unnecessary distractions from Ruby and I make a final check in the mirror to make sure I look my best for her. I notice that I am starting to get a bit of a belly, it probably doesn't help that I've started an addiction to *Cadbury's* dairy milk bars, which according to my mother are a substitute for sex in my life at the moment. Sometimes I really wish my mother was a professor in a subject in something other than psychology so I wouldn't have to have such awkward mother and son conversations.

I push my shoulders back and suck my belly in and stride confidently into the bedroom. As I open the door, I see that Ruby really did follow through on my comment on 'make yourself comfortable', as her dress is strewn on the floor and she is laying on my bed in just her bra and knickers, a lacy cream set which looks absolutely stunning on her, I'm not sure what the Minnie Mouse plaster is all about but I have other things to focus on right now like removing that underwear.

Finally together at last and together forever hopefully...

CHAPTER 23

After walking back to the flat in a dream like state after my time with Ryan, I place the keys in the front door of the shop, ready to head to bed upstairs and deal with the real world the next day. It's 11pm already and I am too tired to deal with Laurence and his betrayal right now, I just hope he is fast asleep upstairs.

Before twisting the lock fully open I realise someone is standing beside me. I squint my eyes as there isn't much light from the street lamps but I can make out the shadow of what appears to be a rather large man who is six feet tall and about six foot wide too, definitely not the build of Laurence or Ryan. I felt my heart race and begin scrambling in my handbag to find my attacker alarm. The shadow then bellows;

'You must be Ruby Samuels. We've been waiting for you. I am PC Jones and this is my colleague PC Barubus.'

As my eyes begin to adjust I begin to see more of the two shadows that are now in front of me. Both PC Jones and Barubus have brown hair styled into a crew cut and look in the mid-forties and both are likely to be categorised as 'larger than life characters'. The police equivalent of Tweedle Dee and Tweedle Dum.

'We need to talk to you about an incident that occurred today at

3pm' said PC Jones, his manner much more serious than his demeanour.

'If it's about that bloody clothes rail it was an accident.'

I immediately cover my mouth, shocked at the way I just spoke to a police officer. If I wasn't in trouble before I am probably in a whole load of trouble now. I never lose my cool with my customers like that yet somehow I have managed to turn into the Queen of Gremlins talking to an officer of the law. I might as well stick my wrists out now for the handcuffs.

Despite the way I have addressed him, he continues to speak in the same monotone manner as before.

'I am not sure what you mean about the clothes rail, we can talk about that later. I think it is best that we go inside and tell you as you may need to sit down.'

Shit. What the hell has happened. Maybe someone has broken into the shop, although there is no sign of any damage or maybe I had inadvertently bought stolen goods, I always thought Marco, the guy I bought tulips from looked a bit fishy, he smelt a bit fishy too but the tulips he sold were always of a good quality.

I unlock the door and turn the lights on before inviting them in. I offer the two police officers a cup of tea, of which they nod in acceptance as they try to find a space to sit amongst the peonies and lavender plants. PC Jones perches on my step-ladder which I use to reach up to the hanging baskets in the shop and PC Barubus decides against sitting and stands precariously by the succulents just a metre away from PC Jones.

Maybe a cup of tea will make them be a bit lenient on me, although what if it is the opposite effect and they are actually setting me up and they see it as bribing a police officer. Don't be silly Ruby, you are overthinking it, no one has made it to the front page of the *Daily Mail* by bribing a policeman with a cup of tea. Offering a cup of tea is about as British as The Queen. I need to calm down.

I try not to shake as I hand the mugs of tea to them. I need to be strong, especially as whatever I have done could soon make me a jailbird, I have seen enough episodes of *Orange is the New Black* to know prison life isn't easy.

'Thank you Miss Samuels,' PC Jones says as he takes a big slurp on his mug. I then realise that the mug I've given him is Catrina's which has on it; 'Don't cha wish your girlfriend was Welsh like me?' Either he hasn't noticed or he is just going to turn a blind eye and mentally chalk up another three months on to the sentence that I will be handed for this thing I have done but don't yet know about.

'Please call me, Ruby. Miss Samuels sounds rather too formal for my liking.'

I am hoping the personal touch will get him on my side, I've seen this type of thing in the movies. It will work in real life won't it?

He gives me a gentle smile, and I feel a moment of relief but in a flash the hard and grave look on his face returns. Oh god, I am in some serious shit right now.

'Okay Ruby. Unfortunately I have some bad news about Laurence Daniels. I believe he was your partner?'

What. The. Fuck. My heart is pounding and my brain feels like it is about to explode. Clearly Laurence was living more of a double life than I knew. I nod my head slowly to confirm he was. Wait… what?! I'm pretty sure he just said 'was your partner' not 'is your partner'. Has Laurence ended this relationship already without having the decency to tell me?

'I am afraid to inform you that Laurence was involved in a road traffic collision early this afternoon and due to the injuries sustained he died at the scene. I am ever so sorry for your loss Miss… erm… Ruby. We've already informed his mother and given her the necessary details, she just asked if we could let you know.'

I stand open-mouthed, unable to take in the words PC Jones has just said to me. I clutch tightly to my mug of tea, hoping that it will somehow give me the strength to continue.

He is dead. Laurence is dead. I can't believe it. I don't want to believe it. I just want someone to pinch me and tell me it's all a lie and that I have time to fix things properly. Despite what happened today, I didn't want him to die. What is happening? I need time alone to process this.

PC Barubus is the first to break the silence that has engulfed the room after the news of Laurence's death.

'Any chance of a biscuit with the tea?'

'Any chance of a biscuit.' Is he fucking serious? This guy clearly lets his stomach do the talking rather than his head. PC Jones has just told me that Laurence, my boyfriend has died and he wants to know if I can find him a biscuit to add to his chances of going into a diabetic coma.

I calm myself down and give him a terse smile and tell him there are no biscuits left as Catrina had had the last one yesterday.

Even PC Jones looked at this colleague in horror as to what he has just asked. He then quickly drinks down the last of his tea, places it on the counter and nudges PC Barubus to do the same.

'Well we better be off now Ruby, as we have quite a busy shift ahead of us. However, if you need any support then just give our Bereavement Officer Bev a ring. She's a lovely lass and can offer you a kind word or two should you need it.'

He fishes out a small business card from his top pocket with Bev's name and number on it and places it gently on my hand as he shuffles out the door, rushing PC Barubus out first in case he says anything else stupid.

As the door slams shuts behind them, I feel numb, alone and confused. I could ring Bev but she doesn't know Laurence like I do and a few kind words aren't going to bring him back and besides after my encounter with PC Jones and Barubus I think I have had enough of police assistance right now.

I just need to wake up out of this dream but I can't because it is reality.

CHAPTER 24

This has been the most confusing eight weeks of my entire life.

Being incredibly callous at least I can say the competition is truly out of the way but I would rather have Laurence alive and be able to fight for Ruby's love fairly and truthfully than see him dead. No one deserves to die. Ever since his death I have seen a change in Ruby. No longer is she the girl who has a sparkle behind her blue eyes instead there is pain and confusion and even when she does try to put on a brave face in front of me.

I am hoping that in time Ruby will get back to herself and be the strong independent person I know. Seeing her so gaunt and frail makes me feel awful inside and I just feel so helpless, all I want to do is wrap her up in my arms and keep her safe from all the pain and suffering she is experiencing.

I have tried my best to comfort Ruby but she feels guilty about having any contact with me due to Laurence. Every time I have held her hand, stroked her hair or offered her the comfort of a warm embrace, she initially takes it and then just as she does she pushes me away as if she was electrocuted.

I do not want to take advantage of her nor do I want to pressurise her into physical contact if she does not feel comfortable. I just want to show her that I love her and I will be there for her. She couldn't have stopped Laurence's death, even though she was near the scene at the time, the impact had killed him instantly.

In a strange way, these dire circumstances have made me much closer to my parents, I even stopped being such a jack ass to Larry; well for now anyway. I still find it grating that he calls me his 'son' when I am a year older than him.

I speak to Mum on the phone everyday now, all that psychology training she has had is actually of use and despite me thinking she had no idea how I lived my life, she knows me pretty well.

She actually gave me some good advice today about the funeral. Although I could've also done with some advice on how to deal with tight underpants at a funeral as despite looking smart on the outside with a black suit, tie and a white shirt, I really feel the urge to rip everything off just to sort out my jocks and get back to feeling comfortable again. Chad must've put these in the boil wash or something as these pants have never been this tight before.

Mum's initial advice was to say 'Is the karaoke after this part?', thankfully she was joking. After she finished howling to herself with laughter as to how gullible I was to think about saying that at a funeral, she then advised me properly and suggested that I should just keep quiet and if speaking to Laurence's parents just say; 'My condolences'. Keep it short and sweet and it prevents any disasters happening.

As I try to subtly rearrange my underwear on the back pew, I look over at Ruby and see that despite her grief, she still looks beautiful. Her curly blonde hair is neatly pinned away from her rosy-cheeked face by a black velvet bow and she has on a long black dress.

Even in such painful circumstances she looks so dignified.

I hesitate as to whether to go over to her or not. I initially wondered as to whether I should be at Laurence's funeral at all as despite exchanging a few words with the guy, he wasn't exactly my best friend and I'm sure he thought likewise, however Ruby had asked me to come as she said that she needed a rock in these unsteady waters.

Ruby must've sensed me watching her as she breaks away from chatting to some elderly guy who might be some sort of uncle or granddad of Laurence's and heads towards me. As she gets within touching distance I feel my stomach begin to flutter, despite everything that has gone on between us she still makes me feel weak at the knees.

She gently places her delicate pale hand on top of mine and whispers in my ear;

'Thank you Ryan for coming, your presence helps makes this whole situation just a little bit… a little bit…'

The softness of her breathe feels comforting against my skin but before she finishes her sentence I feel her hand grip tightly around mine.

Ruby's blue eyes are full of alarm, I turn away from her to see what she is looking at, her hand still tight on mine.

At the church door I see a woman who is about the same age as Ruby wearing a black leather jacket, a black blouse and trousers and some precariously high heels. Her face is covered in a thick layer of make-up and her eyebrows are something to see to be believed. It looks like two well-manicured slugs have decided to camp out above her eyes. She is the epitome of the Essex stereotype. I wonder if she has had a vajazzle done as well?

That thought was totally inappropriate especially at a funeral but with this woman's blouse being rather low cut it doesn't help but bring inappropriate thoughts to mind.

'That's her,' Ruby says through gritted teeth, her grasp getting even stronger.

I look back at Ruby with confusion as to who 'her' is. I've never seen this woman in my life, she isn't someone I would want to spend my time with, even if she might be useful as a paint matcher for painting a garden shed or fence.

'That's Hayley, the one Laurence was seeing.' Ruby's neck is beginning to flush pink, and she looks extremely agitated.

'Get rid of her Ryan.'

The tone from Ruby is venomous, I have never seen her this enflamed before and I know it is a side I do not want to see again. I do as she has requested and hope that I can use some of the old Crichton charm to get Hayley as far away as possible.

I stride over to Hayley confidently, place my hand gently on her right arm and give her a fake warm smile. This was move number one in my Crichton charm book. Make eye contact and ensure you get some sort of subtle physical contact with a girl i.e. gently touch her arm or her shoulder; do not grab her tits as it will land you in all sorts of trouble.

'Hello. You must be lost as I'm surprised to see such a pretty girl like you at a funeral.'

I see Hayley's cheeks pink and her eyelashes are now batting quicker than a pair of windscreen wipers set to max. I'm glad to see that I still haven't lost the magic.

'Hello, errr that's very nice of you to say' she says in a whispery voice as she twirls around her fingers her long ratty extensions, 'but I am here to see Ruby, there is something I need to tell her and also to give her.'

'Well I am sure what you have to say can wait, as you can see she is rather busy at the moment.'

I begin to move just that little bit closer to her to indicate intimacy, another charm trick of mine. She tries to look behind me and catch Ruby's eye but thankfully my six foot frame is stopping her from doing so.

'It's really important that I speak to Ruby now, what I have to say can't wait,' she says pleadingly.

Shit, she really isn't getting the hint. That means only one thing, to resort to the last tactic in my charm book. Lie. Outright lie until you get the girl back to your place or in this case, the complete opposite; get this girl as far away from this place as possible.

'Look, you really can't be here. This funeral is for family only. I don't make the rules but you need to respect Laurence and his family on this. As Laurence's brother tell me what you need to say to Ruby and I will pass the message on to her.'

Well I know where I will be going when I die. Straight to hell. I really need her to get out now because if she speaks to Laurence's parents or Ruby, I might as well book my flight back home and say goodbye to the rest of my life on earth as well.

She lets out a sigh, circles her foot on the tiled church floor and then tips her head back and towards me;

'I never knew he had a brother but it doesn't matter now I s'pose. It looks like I have no choice but to tell you. Please promise you'll pass the message on.'

I nod, crossing my fingers behind my back. She then reaches

206

into the pocket of her leather jacket and pulls out a small black velvet box and places it in my hand.

I feel my heart beating unusually fast as the box rests in my palm and my mind begins to jump to several conclusions as to what this box contains.

'The day of the crash Laurence was paying me a visit, in order to… in order to…'

Hayley is beginning to struggle to get her words out as she is on the verge of crying. Great this is all I need, especially as I was hoping for Hayley to have left by now, no questions asked, instead she wants to start the waterworks.

'Come on now Hayley, there is no need to cry. How about we step outside and take a deep breath and we can continue our conversation.'

I try my best to comfort the girl but my patience is running thin. Thankfully though for the both of us she agrees to my suggestion of standing outside as she could do with a 'fag' to calm her nerves. This girl gets classier every minute.

As we step outside, further away from the danger zone but closer to me getting cancer, a lightbulb moment hits me. I know what this is for. Flat keys. I bet there are keys in this box and Laurence was going to move this dirty slut into the flat and give Ruby the heave ho even though Ruby runs the shop below.

After taking a few further puffs on her 'fag' and me standing like a lemon next to her waiting for her to tell me what's in the box, she then touches my arm for some further sympathy.

'So as I was saying, Laurence came to see me at my shop as he was putting the final touches to this. He was going to surprise her the evening that he… well you know.'

She taps the box that is still firmly clasped in my hand and motions to me to open it, which I do to finally resolve this mystery.

Fuck.

This changes everything. So much for Laurence cheating on her. Ruby can't know about this, it will destroy her. But if I don't tell her it could destroy us. Although if I do tell her it could also destroy us. Fuck fuckety fuck fuck.

In the box is a gold ring on which a large ruby stone sits in the middle with two small diamonds sitting either side.

I cannot believe it, he was going to ask her to marry him. Knowing Ruby she would've have said yes even though she probably would've hated this ring and thought it all rather cliché. Or maybe she would like it, I don't know and I guess we will never know.

I then realise that Hayley is still looking at me with her heavy lidded eyes.

'So you will tell her and give her the ring.'

In order not to raise suspicion and to definitely get her to go away and never come back, I give her the answer she was looking for:

'Yes of course I will tell Ruby, as Laurence's brother I will make sure she gets the message. No need to make any return visits to Ruby, I assure you this will be given to her as soon as possible.'

I can feel the flames of hell already licking at my feet at the gigantic lie I have just told Hayley. Also I hope she didn't picked up on the fact that my voice went up an octave. Despite lying to several women over the years to get them into bed, they have

208

tended to be what I would call small white lies rather than the great big whopping one I have told Hayley.

'Thanks… sorry I didn't catch your name,' says Hayley with a look of relief as she has now passed the burden of this bloody ring to me.

'It's Rupert.'

'Ah okay, thanks Rupert, you are a good man.'

Of all the names I could have come up with, my brain and mouth delivers me Rupert. What kind of normal Australian man is called Rupert. I probably would've been better off with calling myself Bruce, at least that fits an Australian man but then again Laurence wasn't Australian and Hayley didn't pick up that we had different accents or that my name is something from a cartoon strip so I think I got away with it. She didn't look like the sharpest tool in the shed.

Hayley gives me a peck on the cheek and clip-clops her way down the church path to the main road. I breathe a small sigh of relief, glad that this woman has finally left this church and that no one else was involved or saw this conversation. Hayley was also a good reminder of why I gave up the life of chasing and bedding every women in sight, it is too much hard work trying to woo them and then end up getting results that may not be to your satisfaction.

I straighten up my tie and have one more sneaky tug at my trousers to take these fucking undies out of my arse and head back into the church.

As I walk back inside and position myself again in the last row of pews, I see Ruby in all her elegance turn in my direction. I give her a nod to confirm everything is sorted. She lets out a small smile, mouths 'thank you' and her shoulders seem to drop down slightly now that the small problem of Hayley has been dealt with.

I feel a sense of pride that I have helped Ruby but at the same time this ring inside my jacket feels like it is burning a hole straight into my chest.

I spend the service battling with my thoughts as to what I should do about the encounter I have had with Hayley and how I am going to explain this to Ruby, I also feel a pair of eyes are boring into the side of me. As I slowly turn my head to the left I see that it is a figurine of Jesus staring straight at me. If I wasn't feeling guilty before I sure am now. He knows what I need to do and if it was anybody else in this situation they would listen to God's right hand man but I just can't bring myself to do it. I don't want to lose Ruby again.

CHAPTER 25

The words I uttered to Ryan on that fateful day; 'Laurence is dead to me' still cause me so much pain. No one ever deserves to die, especially Laurence he had so much to live for. I let out a loud sob which echoes around the church and feel a comforting hand on my back. It's Carmen. God I hadn't seen Carmen, since I took over her job at 'Fascinating Florals' in Sydney. She must have flown back especially for her half-brother's funeral.

Carmen still looks beautiful despite being in mourning, in fact it suits her very well. She is wearing a lace veiled pill box hat on top of her luscious dark hair and a classic black shift dress. Less can be said for her partner, the one she decided to stay in Oz for. I imagined him to look like David Gandy in a *Dolce and Gabanna* advert and be an absolute Adonis in white underpants. Instead he has a face like a potato and when he shook my hand it felt like I had put my hand in a bag of gravel. All I can say is that he must have a beautiful personality but that seems questionable seeing as he only responds in grunts when people ask him questions.

I'm so glad Ryan managed to get rid of that woman as explaining herself to Carmen and me would make for a rather uncomfortable service. But then if she was Laurence's true love she has every right, to be here and pay her last respects.

Everything is so confusing and I just don't know what to do, the only thing I seem capable of right now is crying uncontrollably.

I wipe my teary eyes and try to gain my composure by focussing on the vicar who is about to begin the sermon. Unfortunately he is the worst type of vicar to conduct this service, with a demeanour more suited to weddings than funerals, he has one of those mouths that even when resting can't help but curl into a smile, a pair of grey whiskers that seem to have gone feral and a pair of moon-shaped glasses, you know the type you find on those classic Father Christmas models that are perched at the end of the nose.

Even his voice had a cheery undertone despite the solemn content of his sermon. It probably doesn't help that his name is Reverend Bright either, although considering the size of his stomach, Revered Rotund would probably be more appropriate. He has clearly enjoyed one too many of the parishioners local bake sales.

Despite the sunny disposition of the vicar, there is a touching tribute from Laurence's mother who gave a beautiful eulogy where I had found out things about Laurence I never knew, such as the time when he was four and decided to hold a teddy's bear picnic in his garden. It wasn't your average teddy bear's picnic as he decided to give the bears a lecture on why they shouldn't be sitting having a picnic with him but should be free and ready to explore the wild like real bears. Laurence was always prepared to be different and was always the first to encourage people to achieve their goals, if it wasn't for him the Lemon Tree would never have become the success that it is.

Even my father, who never seemed to really warm to Laurence stood up on my behalf to do a reading. I couldn't face standing up in front of everyone as I knew I wouldn't have been able to keep my composure with all the lies and hurt I have inside.

212

Dad agreed to do it for me after he saw how much anguish it was causing me yesterday while I was sitting at the kitchen table at their house trying again and again to read the lines but bursting into tears after ever third word.

Dad isn't one for emotional gestures but seeing his daughter get herself in a state must have really got to him as he grabbed me by the arm, pulled me close to him and gave me a warm and embracing hug. Listening to his beating chest and being able to breathe in his smell made me for just a few moments safe and secure. We held our embrace for quite a while before he suddenly whispered in my ear;

'Even mop a tops don't deserve to die.'

I don't think he realised how badly that sentence came out but it did make me break out into a small smile.

***

The service, despite the grinning idiot of the vicar was very touching and I hope Laurence, from his place in the sky above would have approved, despite the fact his love Hayley was shown the door.

When the coffin moved off into the distance towards the crematorium and the curtains finally shut, I knew that was it. Laurence will not be coming back and it is time for me to move on and make the most of every single second I am breathing on this planet. Life is too short not to be lived and to do what you enjoy the most. From this day forward I will make sure to do that even if it means I have to tread my path in life on my own.

CHAPTER 26

It's been a year now. The Ruby I used to know with passion and life burning in her eyes is finally beginning to emerge. There are still days where I see the grey cloud emerge over her head and moments when she sees something that reminds her of him that causes her to take a step back but otherwise Ruby is making progress and prioritising what makes her happy and it is a joy to experience.

I am hoping that now I am 'officially' her boyfriend I can continue to help her on the path of happiness. We've put it on Facebook so it must be official. We decided to wait six months after Laurence's death before announcing to friends that we were 'seeing each other' and slowly building it up to telling people we were now a 'couple'. Chad and Catrina knew what was really going on but as the good friends they are they did not utter a word and besides after the first couple of months after Laurence's death Ruby and I didn't even touch each other, we were more like friends than lovers, we didn't want to be disrespectful to Laurence, even though Ruby still thinks he cheated on her. As we were taking things slowly it allowed me to throw myself into my work especially now that cretin Neil had left, and as a result I have been put forward as a potential partner at Charter and Charter back in the Sydney office, a dream come true but also a slight complication due to my relationship with Ruby and our life here.

I know how hard Ruby has worked to make this a successful business plus I've seen her accounts. I couldn't help it, once an accountant always an accountant. I've offered to help her but this is her little baby and I know from practice it is hard for business owners to let others get involved to shape the business. Whilst she was dealing with a customer I had a sneak look on her laptop at the back at her spreadsheets. There were a few tweaks I would've made to the setup but she has done a pretty good job but I'm always there if she needs me.

Sneaking around on her laptop sounds like I go around and do a lot of things behind Ruby's back but we agreed earlier on that we would share everything and that there would be no secrets, she said Laurence said the same to her and she is trusting me not to let her down on the promise like he did. It's times like this when I should tell her the secret I have harbouring inside, it would take the weight off my shoulders but the thought of losing her forever stops me from telling her the whole truth. I lost her before and I can't go through all that again. He is dead now so there is no reason for the truth to come out.

I pat my left shirt pocket and feel the box heavy against my chest. I keep the ring and the box close to me at all times since Hayley handed it over to me. I have been unsure about what to do with it but a year later I am getting tired of always having to look after it and keep it a secret from Ruby. I'm also concerned that I am going to end up like Gollum and start calling it 'my precious'.

It's time to put my plan into action.

CHAPTER 27

I stare at the reflection in the mirror. I see me. The real me. The twenty-eight year old Ruby who still wears knickers with Snow White on the front. I may be an adult but that doesn't mean I can't still cling on to the Disney dream.

I am proud of this body that allows me to live; the freckles that dance across my nose, the raw red scar on my arm that marks my survival, the curve of my hips and breasts, my milky skin and curly blonde hair. It has taken me a while to love this body but just recently I feel like I am glowing.

Despite glowing on the outside, my insides are a different story as over the past week my stomach keeps wanting to throw out its entire contents into the nearest receptacle. I don't know what is happening, just as I have finally got to a place where I feel mentally and physically stronger from the events that have happened in the last year I suddenly become ill. Although I am wondering whether this sickness is to do with the fact that I binged on several bags of cheesy puffs last week. I couldn't help it, the cravings were just too hard to ignore.

I sneakily bought a multipack bag on Saturday morning whilst Ryan was busy cooking breakfast, giving him the excuse of just checking on the shop below the flat. I carefully opened the door in order to prevent the bell from ringing and creeped out to the nearest corner shop to get my hands on some orange gold.

Despite setting the bell off as I entered back in the shop, thankfully Ryan just thought I was testing the door, I managed to pull out my best ninja moves and get back into the bedroom and close the door without Ryan looking and began stuffing my mouth with the contraband. They just melted so deliciously in the mouth, it was like I had gone to food heaven.

By the time Ryan called me from the kitchen to eat our cooked breakfast I was already three bags down and still wanted more. I then had to do my best to destroy the evidence and any trace of cheesy orange dust across my face and hands. The cheese puffs taste amazing but my god they aren't half messy. As I ran to the en-suite bathroom to destroy the evidence I felt like I was doing the crisp version of Lady Macbeth where she tries to get rid of the blood on her hands; 'Out damn spot'. Or in my case 'Out damn orange stains, for one does not want to use the excuse of a fake tan failure to get out of one's cheesy puff predicament.'

Ryan was none the wiser even though there was a crisp packet sticking out of the bedroom bin, as somehow I still managed to eat some of the bacon sandwiches he had put together.

***

My stomach begins to somersault again and I do my best to vehemently ignore it. I've tried to block out the thought of it being something else that isn't a crisp related illness, something else that I am not quite ready for, something I don't think Ryan will be ready for either.

I glance away from the mirror and over to my alarm clock and see the time flashing at me in bright red. Shit. I'm going to be late. I am due to meet Ryan at the Tate Gallery in 30 minutes but it will take at least 40 minutes to get there. He will not be happy. He was rather adamant that we meet there, in fact he was rather firm in his tone when I questioned him why he wants to meet at the Tate as I didn't realise he was that into art.

I love the Tate, it is my favourite place in London. I remember when our parents first took Martha and I to the gallery, the colours of some of the paintings were so vivid and the sketches and photographs beautifully captured moments in time. Some of the exhibits were completely off the wall and not to my taste but that is the beauty of art, it can be anything you want it to be. It was at that first visit to the Tate as a child that I knew I wanted to do something creative. It led me to grab a pen and paper and find a way to express my feelings and do something I am good at. It is a gift I feel privileged to have and one I need to make more use of in the future. As much as I love floristry it is not my true passion and so over the next few months I hope to take my shop in a direction that reflects my true self.

Martha was less impressed by the Tate when we went and preferred to play on her Gameboy, unsurprisingly she ended up working in the IT industry. So similar in some ways and so different in another. Oh, how I miss my twin, hopefully one day we will be both in the same country and together again.

I look at the alarm clock again and realise I better get going to the Tate before I become really late and Ryan gets all heated up again, although he is quite sexy when he gets all authoritative. I put on my floral tea dress that is beginning to feel a bit snug, quickly powder my face and put on a slick of red lipstick to make myself more presentable followed by some brown sandals. Surprisingly the weather is really sunny today, hopefully a sign of a good day ahead. As I smile to myself as to what adventures today could hold, I feel something rise up again in my throat. I am determined for this not to get the better of me so clench my fists, swallow hard and walk swiftly out of the room to show my stomach who is boss and head down the stairs of the flat to go and meet with the gorgeous human being that is Ryan.

218

CHAPTER 28

'The Kiss' by Auguste Rodin. I look at the sculpture, a pair of naked lovers entwined about to share their first passionate kiss together. I think this should be a suitable spot. I double check around the corner to see if there are any other pictures or statutes that could be suitable to use as a romantic back-drop but other than a wire structure which looks like a scrawling mess made out of my Nan's old coat hangers and some photographs on the wall showing various sketches of women's vaginas, I think this will be the best spot to do something I never imagined I would ever do.

I remember Ruby saying how much she used to love coming to the Tate as a source of ideas for her sketches and how when she first came here as a child how she fell in love with all the different paintings and that this set her on the pathway to become an artist.

I look at the statute again and admire the sculptor's ability to convey such an intimate scene. I just hope that there is no horrific story behind the statute of them dying or find out it is incestual love or something, that would just be my luck that I end up proposing next to something with a dark underlying meaning.

I let out a deep breath and decide to stick with my decision. I am so desperate to get this moment right, for this to be a moment we treasure forever, a moment which will allow us to start a new chapter. I even went all out on the shirt today buying a new light blue long-sleeved shirt from *Versace*. Apparently both Catrina and Chad thought my shirt choice of white, which I wear for work is too 'boring' and my tropical prints for outside work scream 'bachelor party at Vegas'. I always thought I had quite a good sense of style but the raise of the eyebrows of Catrina when I pulled out a short sleeve pink shirt with a hula girl on the front to wear to meet Ruby for our 'special date' suggested otherwise. I refused to tell Chad or Charlie why this date was special despite their continual questioning.

I don't want anyone other than me to know what will make today's date special just in case it goes horrifically wrong. Chad picked up instantly that I was nervous, it was probably the fact that I had literally used half a can of deodorant under each arm this morning to stop the 'nervous sweats'. I also took a few tablets of *Imodium* to prevent me getting the shits too. I know well enough the last time I declared my feelings to Ruby, it felt like the insides of my bowels had left my body several times and I do not want a repeat of that again. I just want everything to be perfect.

Chad just kept telling me before I left to 'take it easy dude and breathe'. It is easy for him to say, he is so laid back all the time he is almost horizontal. I don't know how Catrina puts up with him being so laid back but then I have noticed that when Catrina is around he straightens himself up and ensures that Catrina always feels comfortable. Women. The Achilles heel to men and the biggest contributor to a man's toilet troubles, they are more dangerous than a spicy Vindaloo.

I sometimes wonder whether Uncle Terry had the right idea of just having relationships with men but then again he seems to have become a right miserable bastard since returning from Benidorm with his 'friend' Barry. Every time I speak to Uncle

Terry about Ruby and he would initially show interest but then would tear up, pour himself a large glass of Chardonnay and go into his bedroom playing Tammy Wynette records until 2am in the morning, he has even stopped dressing up as much as he used to, which connecting all the dots together suggests he and his 'friend' Barry didn't quite have the most 'friendliest' holiday as he had hoped.

I've told Mum about it all and her response is that 'little Terry' has always been a sensitive soul. She is due to come over to the U.K. next month so hopefully that will cheer him up. She will also meet Ruby for the first time and I am praying to every deity available that they get along. Although considering she is still with that cretin Larry she can't be too judgmental. She is however looking for new material for her next book and I am hoping she is not going to use mine and Ruby's relationship as the basis for it. I swear I have heard her scribbling notes when I have spoken to her, which is why I have not told her about my special date today.

I fire off a text to Ruby and then begin pacing up and down in front of the sculpture as if I am its own personal security guard. I tell her exactly where I am so she knows where to head to when she arrives. I am hoping she won't be too long as my heart is beating out of my chest and I want to say what I have to say before I turn into a complete pussy and just walk out. I tap my trouser pocket to make sure the box is still there and I hadn't left it on the tube, an unlikely situation considering I have tapped the side of this box nearly every other second on the way here.

I am just hoping people don't think I am trying to touch myself up in public, last thing I need now is someone to scream 'PERVERT!!' and I get carted away before I can explain myself.

I hear a ping from my other pocket and I pull out the phone and see a message from Ruby;

> I've just got to the Tate now. Will be there in 2
> ticks.

My phone almost falls out of my hand due to it being so sweaty and due to Ruby now being only moments away.

I wipe my hands down my black jeans in order to de-sweat them and hope that it doesn't leave a stain. Last thing I want is to look like a sweaty mess in front of Ruby especially as I had to empty most of my bank balance to look this good today.

Suddenly my sight goes and I wonder whether this is it, the pressure of it all has finally got to me. Stress blindness is really a thing isn't it?! Or maybe this is it, just when my life could change for the better, the man above has decided to end it all. Bloody typical.

As I move my hands to my face to see if I can do anything to stop this blindness that has suddenly struck me, I realise it is a pair of hands on my eyes and as I follow the hands I can feel they are attached to a pair of slim and silky arms. I breathe a sigh of relief as its clear I am not taking a trip to see the Grim Reaper.

'So what's the plan Stan?' says a familiar voice booming in my ear. I carefully peel back the soft hands away from my face and turn to face Ruby with a nervous smile.

She looks slightly paler than she normally does maybe it was the drain of the journey from getting from East London to here but otherwise she looks as beautiful as ever.

I begin to stutter;

'Rrruby good good to see you!'

For fuck's sake, I need to get a grip as I am being a pussy with a capital P.

'Are you alright Ryan, you seem a bit off kilter?' Ruby asks concerned.

I'm not sure what she means by 'off kilter', I have never heard of the expression, maybe it's something to do with kilts flying in the wind or maybe I misheard or maybe I am starting to go mad. I can't stand this waiting any longer and the need to build up a conversation before I go in for the plunge and seal my fate, either good or bad. It's time to man up and say what I need to say.

'Ruby, there is something I need to say and do and I am sorry if this offends you or you don't think it is appropriate or its too early or whatever but if you don't like what I am about to do then please be kind to me…'

So much for making this a strong statement.

'What an earth are you on about Ryan? Just hurry up and get on with it.'

I see Ruby clutch her stomach and wonder whether she is getting hangry, not really the best of starts when your girlfriend is getting mad at you because she probably forgot to eat her Cheerios this morning. I better make sure the finale of the event is a good one to make up for how this is going.

I reach for the box in my pocket and I slowly begin to bend down on one knee.

***

The contents of the box were not the same contents as they were before. Previously it held the ring purchased by Laurence, a clichéd ring consisting of a large ruby nestled between two small diamonds and when I say small, if you blink you'd miss them. Not that I should speak ill of the dead but I think he was pretty clueless to her taste.

She may be Ruby by name but that doesn't mean she wants a ruby ring. In fact I subtly asked her after another evenings activity under the bedsheets, if she ever had any ruby rings due to her name being Ruby and the look I received followed by the comment of 'No, I don't want one either as its rather lame', sealed the deal as to the fate of Laurence's ring.

I spoke to Hayley at her shop the next day after Ruby's comments and tried to maintain only eye contact with her despite the fact she was wearing very revealing clothing. No wonder Ruby thought Laurence was up to know good. I explained that Ruby would rather not have anything that was associated with Laurence anymore as it is too emotional for her to deal with. To be honest that probably isn't far from the truth, when a song by The Jam came on the radio in the supermarket a few months ago she put down her half-filled basket and walked straight out of the shop without saying a word. I guess we all handle grief differently but now I think it's time for Laurence to step aside and let someone who is still living and breathing to have their chance of happiness with Ruby.

Hayley seemed disappointed that Ruby wanted to return the ring but her disappointment would never match the feeling of guilt I have inside. I hope I will not be cursed for all eternity for doing this. Somehow Laurence paid for the ring in cash, I'll probably find out that he is part of the Essex Mafia and his death wasn't an accident, the thought made me even more uneasy as I stuffed a whole wad of £50 notes in my jacket, immediately making me a walking target.

I then said to Hayley, after looking over my shoulder twice, I would like to buy a ring for a 'special someone'. I've never seen someone's face change so quickly from sadness to happiness as soon as money had been mentioned.

'So who is the lucky lady then?' she says in her thick Essex accent whilst twirling a piece of hair that once belonged to a poor Romanian teenager.

I just smile and respond with 'just someone special' and keep tight lipped. This nosey bitch didn't need to know anything else. There is no way in hell that I was telling her it was Ruby as I can imagine the reaction I will get, especially as she still thinks I am Laurence's brother.

I knew the ring I wanted, I saw it in the window before I entered the shop. It was a plain thin gold band topped with a large oval shaped diamond centred in the middle of two small opal stones. It was the biggest and brightest ring in the window. A timeless and classic ring which shines brightly, just like Ruby does.

Hayley dutifully put the ring in the small black box the previous ring was in, despite her trying to hide her little cost cutting exercise I could clearly see what she was doing. I decided to let it slide as I didn't want to be in this shop any longer than I had to. Although, after my purchase she can probably go and close the shop for the day if not the week considering how much that ring cost me.

As soon as the ring was in my possession, my body became tense again as I was yet again in charge of something that could potentially be life-changing. I didn't want to lose something that had cost me thousands of pounds and something which I hope will be priceless to Ruby. I popped the box inside my jacket and zipped the pocket up, ready to go home and put the ring in a safe place; my sock draw. However I needed to make the wrong I did before, right.

Further down the high street was a place called 'Motor Mo's', the place where Laurence had bought his scooter. From what Ruby had told me, he adored his scooter, probably almost as much as he adored her so it seemed fitting to speak to Mo and find out about a certain project he had set up last year.

I spotted Mo instantly due to the fact he had 'Mo' written in large red letters on his overalls. He is five foot two inches tall and probably about as wide, with black greasy hair slicked back and an oily residue on his bull-dog like face. As soon as he sees me he greets me with a friendly smile, which relaxes me a little.

'Alwight there sir. Can I 'elp you at all?'

His accent was more Essex than Hayley's and to my Australian ear it took me a while to decipher what he had just said.

'G'day Mo, I'd like to make a contribution to the motorcycle charity you are running, y'know the one that helps those receiving rehab for really bad injuries.'

I sounded like such a fucking douche, for some reason my brain decided to counter Mo's Essex accent with a strong Australian accent.

I opened up my jacket, and pulled out the wad of cash from the inside pocket. Three quarters of which was originally Laurence's along with some cash I also wanted to contribute to the cause. Mo's eyes went wide with disbelief with the amount of money I pulled out of my jacket.

'It's all legit…' I told Mo as I tried to place the cash in to his dirty dinner plate sized hands.

I went from being a walking stereotype for the Australian tourist board to a wannabe Godfather figure.

Mo hesitated and looked me up and down to suss out whether I could belong to the criminal underworld or whether I was playing him a practical joke and that Dame Edna Everage was going to walk out and surprise him at any moment. I think it is clear that I am too much of a pretty boy to be involved with crime so to rule out the other option I decided to quickly explain myself.

'There is about three and a half thousand pounds there, I would like it to be donated anonymously on behalf of my friend Laurence Daniels. I know this would be a cause he would like to have supported.'

Mo's face softens as soon as he hears Laurence's name.

'He was a good boy that Laurence, heart of gold. That's good of you to do that for him. The charity will really appreciate it too.'

He stuffed the money into his overalls and tells me he will put it in the safe and pay it into the charity bank account as soon as possible. He then gives me a bear hug which I wasn't expecting and I tried to act as normal as possible despite my lungs being squeezed to an inch of their life. After giving him several pats on the back as an indicator I really want to be set free he finally lets go and walks back into the heart of the workshop although not before saying;

'Say hello to Kylie for me, when ya next see 'er.'

He then followed this up with a wink and in return I gave him a smile. Although I get asked to say hello to Kylie regularly since living in the U.K., the people asking probably have more chance of seeing her than I will.

***

The events of that day need to remain secret for a while if not forever. Maybe one day I will be in a position to tell the full story to Ruby but not now. I don't want any other person or event to get in the way of my potential happiness with Ruby right now.

So here I am, on bended knee, hoping this beautiful and gorgeous women will want to spend the rest of her life with me. I feel my whole body shake from nerves as I await her response.

I look up at her face to gage her reaction and she gives me a response I was not expecting nor wanted…

A whole load of sick all down my face and shirt.

CHAPTER 29

I am mortified. The moment in a girl's life when she is meant to feel the happiest human being on the planet. Being asked by the love of their life to marry them is something you should cherish and remember forever. It certainly will be something I will remember forever but not something I will cherish. How could I have chundered all over him. I play back the event in my head again and again and wondered whether there was any way I could have stopped myself being sick.

I am sure on YouTube there are many others who are also playing back the event. I don't even want to look on social media right now as there is probably a picture of us on a meme, tweet, video and several Facebook statuses with the hashtag 'epicfail'.

Other than having people laugh and point at us and get their phones out of their pockets to record the event, the aftermath was a bit of a blur. I remember Ryan standing almost in a freeze frame on bended knee not quite sure whether he was having a nightmare or whether he really did have the insides of my stomach running down his face and all over his shirt. I remember looking back at him in absolute horror and my hands clamped across my now beetroot coloured face in case any further fluids decided to escape.

Thankfully Ryan didn't last long in freeze frame mode and being the action man he is, put the ring back in his stained shirt pocket and grabbed my hand. He then pulled me towards the entrance of the Tate blocking out what felt like a hundred pairs of eyes on us and then as we turned a corner he swivelled himself around to face me and told me off like a naughty toddler.

'Right' he barked… 'you head in there', he says pointing to the ladies toilets, '…and I will head in here', pointing to the gents, 'and I will meet you back out here in ten minutes.'

I wasn't sure whether to laugh or cry at that moment in time, although I felt my chance to be Ryan's wife had well and truly gone out of the window, I could not take him seriously as there was a piece of what looked like carrot from last night's roast dinner slowly sliding down his face.

However, I do as I am told and head into the ladies, although I think a trip here is too little too late. I head to the sink, run the cold tap and splash my red face in order to soothe my skin and think desperately how I could salvage the situation.

I know what is making me sick, it's something my Mum said happened to her but this is something I don't want to tell Ryan yet. It's not the right time, in fact I don't feel ready for what's about to happen and part of me hopes that it isn't really happening. But until I know for definite this will have to be a secret. If it is true I will tell him when the moment is right and preferably in a private setting.

I look back in the mirror and tell myself to get a grip and overcome this nauseous feeling and control my stomach. I splash my face with water one more time and push my hands down my hair and dress in order to make myself more presentable and take one final deep breath before heading back out of the door and hope that Ryan hasn't done a runner or is hiding in the toilets out of shame hoping I just walk out so he never has to be associated with me again.

It is only a matter of seconds of me waiting outside the toilet when Ryan also reappears.

He has removed his shirt and just has a very wet white t-shirt on. It shows off his toned body and makes me want him more and I feel my face getting hotter again. He tosses his shirt with disdain in the bin just outside the toilet door. It was an expensive shirt too by the looks of things as the label said 'Versace'. I feel even worse than I did before.

I look up at him with a look of 'I'm really sorry, please don't leave me.' In return he places his hands on his hips and gives me a stern look.

'Only you Miss Samuels, would only cause a scene like that. Don't you think you have caused me enough trouble?'

I don't know what to say, and I feel my eyes begin to sting with tears. Ryan immediately gives me a strong hug and as soon as he grips me with his strong arms, I just crumble completely and make his already wet t-shirt even wetter.

'It's okay honey', he says gently stroking my hair behind my ear. 'I didn't mean to get angry… in fact it's quite funny really'.

We stand entwined together for a few moments until I eventually regain my composure and I begin to wipe my eyes causing the remaining remnants of mascara to stains the back of my hands. I take a quick glimpse of Ryan's t-shirt as we break the embrace to make sure I haven't left a snotty mess on it as I really don't want to be giving any more of his clothes stains today.

He then gets down on one knee again and I feel a surge of happiness in my heart. He may be asking me to marry him outside the Tate Gallery toilets but I don't care, I am glad he wasn't put off by the scene earlier and I still have a chance.

Although there is one thing I need to clarify before I agree.

'Right, I'm going to try this again: Ruby Samuels, will you marry me… and this time I won't take a technicolour yawn for an answer.'

I laugh and say; 'yes but on one condition.'

I see Ryan's eyes droop down and a look of dread as to what this condition is, as if I haven't put this guy through enough already.

'And what is this condition,' he says sternly.

'That you will love me no matter what challenges life brings us.'

'Yes of course Ruby, I will always love you, without you there is no me, through the ups and the downs I will be there for you. And I hope in return you will do the same.'

I nod in return, overwhelmed with emotion and I feel tears begin to fall down my cheeks again, although this time they are tears of happiness.

'Well… I'm still waiting for a clear yes as to whether you will marry me… my knees are starting to hurt a little now…'

I let out a laugh and confirm so loudly with a yes, I again bring undue attention to us. A lady claps after my loud outburst and someone in the distance lets out a whoop but other people just carry on towards the gallery pretending not to notice but sneakily give us a strange look as to why a guy with a rather wet t-shirt has asked a girl who looks emotionally unhinged to marry her in front of the gallery toilets.

This really will be a story to tell the grandkids, if they haven't disowned us by then due to our crazy behaviour.

As Ryan rises from his kneeling position, he grabs hold of both my hands and with our eyes ablaze with emotion, simultaneously say 'I love you'. Further cementing that we are each and others half. I let go of one of Ryan's hands in order that we can make our exit out of the art gallery and begin our new adventure. But first I think I need to buy Ryan a new shirt and as my stomach rumbles, I know I need to get something else... a bag of *Maltesers*... family sized.

ACKNOWLEDGEMENTS

Firstly a huge thank you needs to go to you, the reader. Thank you for going on this second adventure with Ruby and Ryan and I hope you have really enjoyed this read!

As always Mum, Dad, Brother thank you for your unwavering support both book and non-book related. You have kept me sane and strong during these rather peculiar times the world has recently been facing!

A huge thank you also needs to go to my husband, Alex. Just when he thought all the stresses and strains of writing book one was over, I then decided to write another and as always his patience, calmness and just general awesome attitude has made him my rock. Love you more!

After book one I was cautious about writing a second. However there were a group of women who encouraged me to go ahead proving Girl Power is still alive and strong even after Geri Halliwell left the Spice Girls. So a big thank you needs to go to: Sally Shearn, Emma Chapman, Stacy Latto, Ashleigh Lee, Stephanie Law, Amy Haddon, Kirsty Devine, Emma Rumble, all the ladies who worked with me at Crown Law in Wellington, New Zealand – Katie Bykoff, Kelly Frew, Elaine Little, Laura Stanley, Louise Sinclair, Beth Wishart to name just a few. You are all amazing!

A thank you also needs to go to my editor Cressida Downing and the amazingly talented Jessica Bell who designed the cover, you have both helped to give this book some extra shine.

ABOUT THE AUTHOR

Ever since she learned how to read, Stephanie has loved books, so much so that she decided to begin writing her own books full of fun, love and adventure.

Stephanie has written for a variety or publications in a non-fiction capacity, both in the UK and Australia and is keen to venture further into the world of fiction.

When not putting pen to paper you can find her trying to grapple with the law or stuffing her face with chocolate buttons.

To keep up to date with the latest news and publications from Stephanie Cross, connect via the following channels:

Instagram: @s.crossauthor

Web: www.itsdefinitelystephanie.com

ALSO BY THIS AUTHOR…

'She's like Jackie Collins but without the money' – Stephanie's boyfriend (now long-suffering husband)

'It's like 50 Shades meets Coronation Street' – Stephanie's Mum

Available to buy on Amazon now.

www.ingramcontent.com/pod-product-compliance
Lightning Source LLC
Chambersburg PA
CBHW050616190726
48283CB00007B/2440